About *Arimathea*,
also by Frank McGuinness

'[I]nvested with weighty, parable-like intensity.'
— *Times Literary Supplement*

'A work of passion and truth, in which imaginative
daring is matched by deep psychological insight.'
— Declan Kiberd

'[A] powerful, passionate novel ... quirky, authentic,
often humorous voices.'
— *Books Ireland*

'[A] distinctively Irish book ... echoes of Joyce.'
— *The Irish Times*

Frank McGuinness is Professor of Creative Writing at University College Dublin. A world-renowned, award-winning playwright, his first great stage hit was the highly acclaimed *Observe the Sons of Ulster Marching Towards the Somme*. His other plays include *The Factory Girls, Innocence, Carthaginians, Mary and Lizzie, The Bread Man, The Bird Sanctuary, Mutabilitie, Someone Who'll Watch over Me, Dolly West's Kitchen, Gates of Gold, Speaking Like Magpies, There Came a Gypsy Riding, Greta Garbo Came to Donegal, Crocodile, The Match Box, The Hanging Gardens*, and a musical play *Donegal* (with music by Kevin Doherty). Adaptations of classic plays include Lorca's *Yerma*; Chekhov's *Three Sisters* and *Uncle Vanya*; Brecht's *The Threepenny Opera* and *The Caucasian Chalk Circle*; Ibsen's *Hedda Gabler, A Doll's House, Peer Gynt, The Lady from the Sea, John Gabriel Borkman, Ghosts, The Wild Duck* and *Rosmersholm*; Sophocles' *Electra, Oedipus* and *Thebans*; Ostrovsky's *The Storm*; Strindberg's *Miss Julie*; Euripides' *Hecuba* and *Helen*; Racine's *Phaedra*; Molina's *Damned by Despair*; and dramatisations of James Joyce's *The Dead* and Du Maurier's *Rebecca*. Television screenplays include *Scout, The Hen House, Talk of Angels, Dancing at Lughnasa, A Short Stay in Switzerland* and *A Song for Jenny*.

Awards include:
London Evening Standard Award for Most Promising Playwright, Rooney Prize for Irish Literature, Harvey's Best Play Award, Cheltenham Literary Prize Plays and Players Award, Ewart-Biggs Memorial Prize, London Fringe Award, New York Critics' Circle Award, Writers' Guild Award for Best Play, Best Revival Tony Award, Outer Critics' Award, Prix de l'Intervision and Prix de l'Art Critique at the Prague International Television Awards.

His first novel, *Arimathea*, was published by Brandon/The O'Brien Press in 2013.

FRANK McGUINNESS

THE WOOD CUT TER

AND HIS FAMILY

BRANDON

FOR PHILIP TILLING

Contents

CHAPTER ONE

Son

Archie

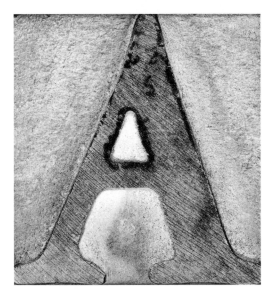

Zurich, Switzerland

On the day I was born my father set himself the task of learning to lip-read. Why a man so prodigiously talented in the acquisition of the earth's languages should undertake such a challenge has always and ever baffled me. Perhaps it baffled himself. Who can say?

He never spoke of it again, so it fell to my mother to confess this strange feat many years after he had committed himself to this pursuit. There was no necessity for it. None of us was deaf, and neither was any of his family dumb. Did he wish us to be?

Could that be what he was looking for, silence? The great man of letters, celebrated the globe over, did he above all else wish to escape from our chattering and retreat where nothing could trouble him but his meanderings and motives, known only to his own sweet self? I cannot tell you an answer to that, for I failed to ask him when he was hale and hearty enough to reply. It was one of many failures which he forgave me. Indeed he forgave us all without complaint, no matter how many times we had let him down – in thought, in word, and in deed. The most benevolent of famous men, Papa.

He forgave that I was born too early. Poor Mama had such a fright. She'd firmly maintained I would not arrive until the end of August. Even September. When she started to feel sore and sick in her stomach, she cursed what she'd had for breakfast. I blame the Famine, the Irish Famine, she said, I blame it for everything that afflicts us as a race, but more than anything I blame it because I can never ever waste a morsel of food, and the consequence is I have nearly poisoned myself on numerous occasions, forcing down rancid meat a rat would not digest, and that's what I did this morning, choosing not to throw into the bin a slice of ham but instead smothered it in butter between two bits of bread and convinced myself it was fit to eat. Look at me now, poisoned – all my own fault, don't pity me.

Father didn't.

And he was not going to encourage her to rant further on the Famine. It was one of her dominant topics of conversation. She could link it to every misfortune that befell our family – even Hitler. I cannot for the life of me remember how she forged a precise connection between the two, but can recall that, when she did, Papa told her she was the most ridiculous woman he'd ever married. She burst into tears as he was correcting himself and said he meant met, not married.

She took this to imply that all the years he'd kept her from a state of wedlock, they had nothing to do with his hatred of the Catholic sacrament but were merely another way of humiliating an innocent poor Galway girl who'd abandoned all to serve him, the dirty Dublin rogue.

You only wanted me for my stories, she accused him. No, he corrected her, it was to save you from the Famine. That would have been a kindness years ago in 1845, she said, are you implying I am over a hundred and I look it? Yes, he said, if it pleases you. It didn't.

A similar row was threatening to develop on the day of my birth, 27 July. I mentioned the ham she had been wolfing, didn't I? But did I let slip that my father had no intention of staying with her that day? No, he'd planned to go swimming, and she'd happily let him, because he always returned in peaceful mood; immersion in water seeming to placate him, as if he'd endured another Baptism, welcomed into the fold of civilised men who could show a modicum of respect to their wives. Go on, enjoy yourself, I am fine, she informed him. He believed her for there was not a chance in hell she was in labour.

But she was. As soon as Papa closed the door, she knew it for sure, yet would she give him the satisfaction of calling him back to convince him why she was so certain? How many babies had she seen born in the west of Ireland? How many women had she witnessed in the throes of their agony? Strong, strapping lassies, full of devilment and laughing fit to burst their sides. Well, boyo, birthing put a stop to their smiling.

Still, she maintained she was cut from Connemara granite. She was no soft caramel. She could endure it. And she prayed he would come back to be with her. Prayed to the Virgin most pure, Star of the Sea, pray for the wanderer, pray for me. And whether it was indeed the Virgin worked her miracle and let him hear, or whether it was he found a hole in his red swimming costume that rendered it indecent, back he came to the second-floor flat, Via S Niccolo, 30, Trieste, to find her in deepest agony. He called for the landlady, Signora Canarutto, to assist them like a good woman – for the love of the divine Jesus, my mother added, forgetting in the panic the Signora was Jewish.

Not that such things mattered in times of this nature, although when we'd last crossed the border into Switzerland my father had to convince the relevant authorities we were indeed Aryan. A long way down the line of my life till that would happen. Now the necessity was to make preparations for my birth. The presence of my papa and her neighbours calmed my mother, she said. All her life her greatest dread was that she would die alone, or, more specifically, that she would bleed to death and no one there to stop the flow. She felt sure now she would not have to endure such a death. Hence, she was more than content to let everything be done for her. Quite the lady of leisure, am I not? she joked. No one found it funny.

Of course the midwife must be in attendance, and so they fetched her, a Giuseppina Scaber. She looked like a reverend mother, but not one to put the fear of God in you, nor had she the look that, at a moment's asking, the devil and all his demons would possess her and allow her tear you limb by limb for having the cheek to pry into what was not your business by asking for something – anything – to relieve your pain.

No such relief was forthcoming, and my mother told me she would not complain, because it was right and proper a mother be tough enough to tolerate whatever spasms, twists and turns of torture her child in the womb inflicts for its pleasure on her, since the infant is only fighting to be free and into this world, roaring its lungs out. She kept changing specific details as to how I had conducted myself through these hours of labour. The last time she talked of that day, and she does often, it would seem I leapt piping out of her, revelling in the light, beaming at the sun. I have never known a little one more in love with the first day of his existence, she'd observe, and my father, he would say, then it is a pity the same bambino was not able to settle the quarrel where the bed should be.

In Italy there is always a row brewing, and Trieste prides itself on providing its citizens with the best of rows. Something in the air, the water, or even the bread – maybe all three – ensure tempers are explosive. At first everything seemed methodical and calm, though since my mother thought there was at least another month before she would be due at the end of August, nothing really had been prepared. But Signora Canarutto was Italian, she had in her permanent possession all that could be necessary and needed for the birth of a baby. These were quietly summoned and assembled. No chance of anything going amiss. But she did not like where the bed was placed, and so much furniture surrounding it. Things must be moved.

My father was foolish enough to resist, or at least to ask why. The Signora explained that the bed had to be moved to the centre of the room, since, many years ago, it had been brought from Jerusalem. My father did not follow her reasoning. It was quite simple. As every civilised person knew or agreed upon, Jerusalem, the city of God, was the centre of the earth. So it was very important, for all manner of things, that the bed carved there centuries ago and brought by her family at great discomfort and expense no matter where they wandered, this bed must be given pride of place at all great events. The Signora had specifically placed this beautiful object in my parents' apartment to encourage their fertility, and it had not failed them, as, for generations, it had not failed her own.

Do you mean to say, my father foolishly argued, that myself and my wife, both of us healthy as Irish trout, are only having this baby because of your bed? The Signora excused herself for her ignorance, but could he enlighten her what a trout, Irish or otherwise, had to do with this conception and delivery of a new baby? Perhaps it did, my father mused. Perhaps we were more wanton in the days of Noah's Ark than we realise or remember. Perhaps man, woman and child were fucking fish, as there can't have been much else to pass the time on that endless sea voyage. Perhaps we can, if truth be told, trace our descent from a single herring or salmon, and that we are all family beneath the fin.

The Signora was not sure how, but felt she was being mocked. She was certain of it when he made his next speculation. This bed, this bed elaborately carved with mermaids, with doves, with fish, even a sail – might it not be part of the timber with which aeons ago Noah made his boat? Strange things have happened, stranger things survived. Here was where our species found the necessary push and shove, the Brace yourself, Bridget, all Irish men declare to their wives before the ride – they say it all over Roscommon, my mother informed us – this bed had evolved from the boards of that celebrated ark, could it be possible? My father asked the landlady would this be a question to perplex her rabbi?

That's when she was certain he was ridiculing her. She took no more action than to tell him it was time to join her menfolk for his evening meal and leave what work had to be done by the women. Go down now, go down instantly, there is enough food, she urged him. He offered first to give a hand moving the bed to the centre of the room as she required, but she abruptly refused, claiming it was essential only the women perform this task. My mother pointed out the heaviness of the bed, but she was scorned as a weak female. A female on the verge of giving birth, Mama retaliated, but the Signora simply observed, in her experience, pregnant ladies all had vivid imaginations and liked to fancy they suffered from every disease under the sun – hypochondriacs, that was the word she searched for. Now, she ordered, come along, put your shoulders to it, get this bed into the centre of the room.

The three of them – Mama, midwife, landlady – did so, Mama occasionally howling when one birth pang struck her more severely than others. A look from the Signora silenced her, but she was a happy woman to collapse onto the mattress, open her mouth and yell the house down at the agony in the garden she was now enduring for my sake, for my father's sake, for his father and all the fathers who walk this earth, bestowing her curses on each and every man whose cock found its way where it had no business being, damning her son, if son I should be, emerging from her womb, to be sterile, fearing to look at a woman, let alone touch one, wishing her own mother had taken a stick the day and hour she was born herself and lashed the life out of her so that she would not have to suffer the torments of hell burning in her belly. Fetch the father, she screamed, so that I can strangle the whore's whelp that has done this to me, I will crucify him on the Claddagh, roast the flesh off his bones on Taylor's Hill, eat him alive through the quays of Galway, give him to me.

All this, she told me, for the pain had imprinted every word on her memory, and if she didn't recall each word, who would? Indeed, the midwife told Mama afterwards she had been a very brave and very beautiful girl who dealt with all she'd had to suffer in a most calm and dignified manner, enduring her turmoil with true grace and devout belief in the knowledge this ordeal must pass. The landlady backed up that story, and this, I believe, must account for the confusion in Mama's versions of my birth – how she could be at times so confident I had slipped into the world without effort or anger.

But maybe something had gone amiss. They did decide to send for a doctor, Sinigaglia, a pupil of English with my father. My mother has no recollection of a man being in the room other than a male voice wondering what it could be she was speaking when she found she was blathering to herself in what was most likely remnants of Gaelic that had lodged themselves from schooldays in her mind and would never be budged – maybe the chorus of an old song, or the Angelus they said at midday, always recited in the ancient language, an act of defiance against the English. She had gone beyond the limits of agony when my head started to emerge, and I was there, alive, welcomed, whole, into the world.

My mother wept with joy, with relief, and when Dr Sinigaglia told her I was a boy, she clapped her hands with happiness. He had not heard her diatribe against his sex, so he put this joy down to her desire she would mother a son. The midwife Scaber, she heard the applause, and my mother said she will never forget the smile they shared at their little secret. I asked her did she really mean those terrible names she pinned on me and Papa, and she assured me of course not – if she had been in earnest, she would never have let me in on what she'd said in the heat of her agony. Anyway, why was I questioning her, when she kept up the story of how little trouble I'd actually caused her, coming into this family?

Mama had this gift of causing confusion. I never knew when to believe her. My sister, I knew, never spoke the truth – she simply couldn't. My father could only tell you the same story in sixty different versions, being averse to any single way of giving a body the beginning, middle and end of a tale, a habit inherited, he said, from his own father who never trusted any being that could not believe both sides of the same story, and Grandfather could invent as many more sides of a yarn as were necessary to account for all the dimensions you could desire. It must, you might have imagined therefore, have been some hullaballoo to come up with a name for myself, their firstborn, the carrier of all their hopes and dreams. Were there ructions deciding?

There weren't any.

Archibald, for my father's little brother, who died years before. Archibald, Archie. Mama agreed to this, without quarrel. She knew how much my father lamented the loss of that child, my uncle I suppose. Knowing her as I do now, I am surprised she did not murmur some objections, fearing that I would be haunted by a spirit, or that some ghostly presence might find its way inside me just for the hell of it. No such phantom was sighted, the dead boy remained in his grave. My father had his way in all respects concerning this affair, even so far as to Mama agreeing I would not be christened. Again, she surprised Papa. He expected at least a small confrontation, but none materialised.

With my mother, this might arouse suspicion, but it didn't. He really should have comprehended that by offering no apparent resistance, she was resisting most fiercely. I caught wind of this even at a very early age when it suddenly dawned on me she could call me by another name than Archie, and this would prove to be her revolt against Papa. She would at times take an age to comb my hair, lovingly stroke every strand, kiss my scalp a thousand times and, on very rare occasions, whisper into my ear, lest anyone should catch her, There now, Michael, that's you grand. I let this happen a few times before I cottoned on there was no Michael there – could not possibly be anyone but myself, so like any nosy little boy, I asked her, Who is Michael, Mama?

I remember this because it was the first time in my life I felt shock move through another human being. I could feel her body – do what? Sway? Stiffen? And I repeated my question, Who is Michael? She laughed out loud in a way I now, of course, recognise meant we were to share a secret I must at all costs keep from Papa. I would not be hushed, though. Who is – and before I said the name, she'd put her finger to my lips to silence me from saying it. Michael, he is your guardian angel, she told me, and a fine swagger of a celestial being he is, there at all times to protect little Archie and keep him safe. I can't see him, I told her, and again she laughed out loud. Well, naturally you can't, she explained, nobody is permitted to see their own, but I can see and speak to him when he allows me to. Is he beautiful? I inquired. Very much so, the picture of beauty, and pale, so pale as if his skin had never seen the sun, and I like pale men, she explained, they have the touch of death about them, God forgive me saying the like.

Does Papa see him too, the angel Michael? I innocently asked her. She tugged at my hair, hurting me a bit, taking her time before she answered. There is one thing I want you to promise me above all other promises, and if you are a good boy, you will do this – are you my good boy? she asked. I am your best boy, I assured her. Then you must never, ever let a word of this slip out when Papa is here; it is to be our big secret, and you will never let him know of it, do you swear that? she demanded. I nodded, but wanted to know why. Does Papa not like angels? He doesn't believe in them, she explained, he doesn't want us to believe in them either, and if he hears us talking about them, he will be very cross. Do you want to make Papa very cross? I assured her I didn't. Good, she sighed, and I was delighted I had pleased her.

I have spent my life trying to please both of them, the parents I love but who have been very difficult people, I must admit. Their ins and outs, their whys and where-fores, they have exasperated me many, many times. With the pair of these Irish tearaways – as they both are in their very separate cases – it is as if I have been beating my head against a most resistant brick wall, one as resolute, as stubborn as the other, each knowing precisely how to infuriate a nation, as Mama sometimes says of Papa, but it is just as true of her. I try to keep the peace between them, frequently to no avail, but it is how I am and they let me do my best to appease them, without listening to me. My sister, though, my sister …

Sometimes she opens her mouth and screams. It is to stop them quarrelling, she used to claim, but now I fancy she does it just because she can and everyone must stop and listen to what exits from that roaring mouth of hers. If Papa meant it when he said he would study lip-reading, I wonder what would he make of the sounds that erupt from his deafening daughter? They each blame the other for her capacity to make our ears bleed. Your father, Papa taunted Mama, you said he had a knack of tumbling the walls of any dirt cabin if he thought he would get a drink to shut him up. Weren't those the very words I heard you use when you yourself, my precious wife, were three sheets to the wind and proved you had a thirst to match his? Christ look down on me and forgive us all, you have a memory like an elephant and a hide like one to taunt me in this fashion, she rampaged against him. Have I not got a struggle enough on my hands dealing with that one's fantasies and fancies without you rubbing my nose in her madness and blaming me and my breed?

That word stopped all consternation. That subject. Madness. It was used only in the most extreme circumstances. That was the rule. And as a rule, it had proved effective though nowadays it seemed to be spoken at the drop of a hat. Still and all, Papa never rose to the bait. If he might be expected to draw himself to his full height and let rip a volley of facts and figures that could prove where these streaks of lunacy stemmed from that afflicted us, then on this occasion he could not be drawn into open warfare. Best to let things stand, my mother decided – his silence alone exhausted her tonight. Were she to get into a slagging match, her head might explode.

Not that anyone would notice if it did. This would be her parting shot for the evening, but she was unprepared for my request. I asked because somehow I sensed – don't ask me why – I would be given whatever I craved, as some way to appease me for enduring my sister's screams. Can I have a birthday party? I looked at both of them. A birthday party, I repeated, and invite friends? Why are you looking for this? Mama demanded to know, you've never insisted before. Because I want to, I told her, but if I cannot have it on the exact day – if that date is not convenient for you, I don't mind waiting, I can be patient, I spelt out to her, even for a few months – until September, the end of September, and I smiled at Papa. Why then – why wait till then? Because it is the feast day of my favourite saint – my favourite angel. St Michael.

My mother gave her loud laugh, with all the workings of the world buried in it. Could you be up to him, this fellow? Now it's the saints and angels he wants to associate with – is that right, Archie? I tell you, she pointed at Papa, you've made a fine fist of an atheist out of him. At so tender an age, already he's in communion with your enemies. Who learned him of feast days and the like? Don't look at me. I have only been following your strict orders to keep silent on all such matters so their heads are not turned astray with such superstitious nonsense as you have declared I was taught and you were taught at your mother's knee. Have I not had that lesson hammered into me so hard didn't I agree my child – my son – would not be baptised at your bidding? Who's the dictator–

You have had him christened, he said, don't deny that; bad enough his mother subjected him as an infant to that ignominy, without her being a liar as well.

How could I be lying? When did I do it? she asked. Are you saying I arranged for him to get the sacrament behind your back? A midwife can bless a baby in danger of dying, he retorted. So you are now calling me some low class of wet nurse? I'll pass on that appellation, she demurred, though I admit the language you subject me to hear should not be uttered in a lady's presence. Better fit for you to be saying your prayers.

But she got no further, for he thumped the table, shouting, I've got you now, you've walked into it, you did what I accused you of doing, you had my son—

Circumcised? I did not, she denied, for I regard that as a vile and cruel act against a tiny little fellow, and look at you, a grown man touching yourself where you shouldn't, as if I'm going to come with a knife or a nettle to sting the jizz out of you before chopping you clean.

I could never anticipate what they would find hilarious. It must be something secret shared between only the two of them. But this was one occasion when she had him in fits of laughter. He was holding himself as if his sides would split open. If they did, I imagined what would pour out of them – and for some reason I thought it might be chickens.

Not china or chocolate hens but real ones, with feathers and scaly feet and eggs that didn't break when they landed on our floor. Where did that come from? Something he'd said – something he pictured in his mind's eye and passed it on to me, one brain leeching into the next, father to son? I never asked him, for I doubt if he'd answer, and he can't now, lying there, waiting to die, to let go and stop listening, stop speaking, stop gabbling, stop writing. My father is a great writer, but you wouldn't think it if you'd just recently come across him. It's tempting to say that now at the quiet end of his days he's keen to keep his counsel. It's not true. He's just tired. Exhausted. Worn to the bone. He always was. It was why he missed my party. Or threatened to.

There was cake, of course. In the shape of a clock, the hour hand pointing to my age, and the date iced on the centre of the face. This did not please my mother. She had asked for the date to be at the side, month on the right, day on the left. I thought she might relent and let the day go off peacefully. My father told her the fuss she was making over nothing was spoiling the celebration for me. She replied she had paid good money for what she'd specifically ordered, and it was not satisfactory that the bakers had failed to deliver. She had a good mind not to pay. That is how her family always dealt with the best of tradesmen Galway had to offer. By not paying them? Papa teased her, but she was not for stopping this time.

I think you'll find that's more your family's failing — a bit of an allergy to settling bills, she retaliated. Jesus, if we had sixpence for every time your shower had to make a midnight flit round the streets of dirty Dublin, I'd be sitting dripping in diamonds. Don't dare upcast, in my direction, we didn't pull our weight in Galway. My people could face the highest and the lowest in the land knowing we owed nobody as much as a sixpence. You get what you pay for — an old saying and a true one of my grandmother's. I said what I wanted to them baking this cake, I didn't get that — in fact, as far as I'm concerned, I got nothing, so that's what I'll offer them. Let them sing for their money.

My father paid for the cake. She didn't resist. You take the good out of everything, he chided, look at the poor child's face, shattered. You've ruined the day that's in it.

All right, she declared, for his sake I'll cheer up, I'll welcome his pals, the merry band of men, not one of whose parents would clean their arse with us if opportunity of such misfortune we'd meet should arise. Stop talking like that in front of the boy, he demanded. Why? she asked, hasn't he heard much worse spewing from your filthy mouth?

I had.

It was fortunate so few of my school friends could speak any English, for there were times when some oaths and choice phrases learned from listening to both of them spilt from my lips, each accusing the other of being the source of my foul tongue. Where did your learn that mouthful? I'd be quizzed by either. I was cunning enough to catch Papa out and just tell him what he wanted. When she was in a temper, Mama would accuse me, you have neither your father's brain nor the brawn of the men on my side of your breeding, what's to become of you if we don't leave you money? Not that there's much chance of that. We have had to scrimp and save to give you this treat, so you'd better enjoy it, she threatened.

The boys came in their Sunday bests, red bow ties, little suits, socks neatly matching their black polished shoes, myself rigged out like the rest of them. Each shook my hand politely and handed me a small gift – balloons, a few books, a yellow candle for some reason or other, and, I now remember, a spinning top. I already had a smaller one, made from tin, but this was wooden and painted the colours of the Union Jack. Go on, Archie, spin it, my mother told me, and, as I recall, I did, making it whirl in the silence as we watched it rotate and rotate and rotate until it fell lopsided by my feet. Are you not supposed to make a wish on your birthday? Mama asked. What would you wish for, son?

Could I tell her any of the many things I so wanted to happen? That my sister would disappear and I would again be their only child? That I could learn the piano well enough to please Papa? Sing more beautifully to make Mama cry with pleasure and smile as if her cheeks might crack with happiness? Or be the smartest boy in the class, scoring top marks, and that way some of my schoolmates – if only one of them – might like me? For even here, at my birthday party, swimming with good things and ice cream, none of them really spoke to me. Yes, they were polite, particularly to Mama, courteous and well behaved, but they addressed their questions and answers only to each other, never to me.

Now I had no cause to complain. I was too shy to start a conversation with any. If they were ignoring me, it was because they were paying me back in the same coin as I had dealt them. And yet I was surprised my brilliant plan of taking them into our house and letting them enjoy my birthday had so backfired. If I had been lonely in their company up to now, then I would be ten times more so after today. Mama must have noticed how little rapport there existed between me and the others. She suddenly clapped her hands and said it was time for games. This provoked some cheers, not terribly hearty, more like an acknowledgement that this turn of events was to be expected, best get it over with.

Who will hide and who will seek? Mama decided: Archie and your friend – what's your name? Federico – Federico then, hide with Archie, she commanded, the rest of you, come with me, outside to the landing and let them find a dark corner to confuse us. She marched the boys out, and Federico gave me a look of more than usual utter contempt.

– I don't know where it would be healthy to hide in this pigsty, he declared, but if it should be necessary to squeeze in, please do not touch me.

– My home is not a pigsty.

– It smells of you, it stinks of pig, it stinks of sties. I am only being polite, in front of your mother, that I did not vomit in her presence.

— You are not polite, you are very rude, Federico.

— Yes, Archie, perhaps I am, perhaps you deserve I should be. What kind of name is Archie, anyhow?

— It is a family name.

— Not your father's name? Is it a Jewish name? Are you Jewish?

The way Federico said that, it was like a blow in the stomach. He was eyeballing me. I was so taken aback I could not answer. Then I heard my mother calling from outside, wondering if we'd found a hiding place. Not yet, I called back. Well, hurry up, she admonished.

Federico was climbing under a table. That's too obvious, I assured him, they'll find us first thing. That is what I'm hoping they'll do, he snapped back, get under. I did as he bid, and when the pack entered, I heard myself hissing at him, we aren't Jewish, none of us.

— Your Papa does not go to Mass or take the Sacraments?

— No, he doesn't.

— Neither does your Mama?

— Neither does she.

– Why not? Do they not believe in good God? Or do they only believe in the Jewish gods?

His hand went to my trousers and I felt him rapidly unbutton them. Boys were searching all through the bedroom's presses and wardrobes, some even rolling under the bed. Federico had found the gap in my underwear and with some dexterity squeezed my dickybird tight. Now the gang were turning their attention to the table.

I could feel my stomach churning as he rapidly left me alone. Do up your buttons – do it quickly, he ordered, and I did so just as they snatched the cloth from the table to reveal us, him innocent as the day is long, cheering their discovery of himself and myself, me burning like the sun, breathless as if I'd run the whole way from school.

I saw where my mother had perched herself, and where she must have stood since coming back to the room. Right beside the table, hearing everything, saying nothing, daring me to tell her what we had been getting up to in the dark, and I was so overwhelmed with relief Papa was nowhere in evidence, for in ways I believed I had done to him something as wrong as Federico had done to me.

From that day on, though we said nothing, Mama would

use what she learned as a threat. When I upset her, or asked for something that pained her or she did not like to give me permission to do, she would sigh and raise her eyes, saying, should we not ask Papa? She was, I felt, ever allowing me to know this could be the occasion when she might let slip what his son enjoyed doing, playing hide and seek with his friends under a table.

Even now as he is dying, is she capable of telling him? Do I want her to whisper all the secrets she and I conspired to share? For all his fame, we – his wife, his boy – we kept so much from him. At whose instigation? Her? Me? The two of us?

I cannot say for sure, and neither can she. Tonight, all these years later, she suddenly returns to that birthday party, remembering the delicious cake – was it chocolate? she asks. I think it was, I lie. And did it have birds flying on it – in icing? she wonders. It may have had, I tell her, I can't say. She wants to know did we eat chicken or veal? There was only cake, I inform her, and ice cream, buckets of ice cream. She asks what became of them? Those boys who attended the party? Do you ever see any of them? There were so many I doubt if I'd know where they disappeared. I let her understand that none of them was very special to me.

One of them, a dark haired boy, what was his name? The best-looking, do you remember him? she wonders. Federico, I tell her, yes, I do. What became of him? He is fighting in the army, the Italian army, I say. I hope he is safe, she sighs. He will be, his type always are, I tell her. What type? she wants to know. My father saves me. From his bed he says my mother's name. I know they are going to speak of my sister, or of dying, and I wish only to escape from either subject, so I excuse myself, saying I need fresh air.

Is such air to be found in Zurich? It is a city – in fact, the only city – where I find my lungs congest and I have to gasp for breath. Why this should be the case I struggle to discover. The people do not suffer from any lack of friendliness. By and large, they are distant but amiable enough, with splendid Swiss manners. So why then is it such an effort to walk through the streets and not feel as if I will soon expire, panting like a fish longing for salt water? And perhaps the explanation can be found when I remember another oddity – why, no matter where I intend walking, is my destination always the graveyard, where Papa will be lying, sooner rather than later? What wicked motive could be stirring deep in my brain? Am I urging him on his way and do not even realise how much I desire—

Yes, my desires, always a problem. Never satisfied, never realised, perhaps best not. As a family we have tended not to share our infatuations with the common lot of humanity. In my case this oddness first manifested itself fully when as a small boy in company with Papa, we visited my mother's mother in Galway. Just the two of us, the menfolk – some quarrel or other, between mother and daughter, there was constant bickering in that quarter, prevented Mama from travelling that time with us back to Ireland to see her family. She would not give them the satisfaction of being first to relent once again and break breath to such a gang of shysters, as she might describe them. But they received us – the swanky, foreign boys all the way from Italy – most kindly, with a comfortable bed to share in my grandmother's house and jars of sweet, milky tea that I revelled in like the best of all Connaught gallants, devils for the sup of the soft stuff. Those nights were my happiest, ever deep in my father's arms, no one else to disturb our sleep. And during the days, I spent my time pursuing my first love – the most beautiful swan eyes were ever set on, that was agreed by all.

My grandmother panicked at my fascination with this creature. She knew too well the strength of such birds. Hadn't a cousin of her own had his arm broken, a full-grown man, when in a moment of daring-do he ventured too close once to a nest. The swan beat the lining out of him, and though in company she held her tongue, my grandmother was on the side of the feathered fellow. Wasn't the poor darling only trying to protect its young? Who wouldn't lift a hefty wing and let fly with it, should such a weapon be in the vicinity of your fist or beak or whatever was appropriate in a fight? The woman then sensed I'd have a connection with this Hercules of the sky, inheriting, through her, an affinity with its ways and means. Best put a rapid stop to that carry on, but she was too late. It turned out the swan adored me, and I took to it.

What else could I do, so handsome and winning as it was? It walked beside me, like a pet dog. If any dared come near me, it would go most viciously for them, reserving a special savagery for my grandmother. She thought this the funniest thing in the world, complaining to the swan it was a most ungrateful beast, since she and she alone stood up for it when the cousin endured the full brunt of that strength, and he would see it put down if given a gun.

I know who's behind it, she whispered, I know who's hidden inside it, it's your mother, my most unforgiving daughter, she's crept within the skin to keep the evil eye on us, and her raging we're having the time of our lives just to spite her. Well, let her stew. I have no fear of the same lady, and I don't fear the swan that serves her.

What did I care if that was the case? As far as I could make out, I was far from Mama's scheming, no matter what others made of my swan. At night it would turn into my Papa, and we would fly above the bed out the open window, over the great city of Galway and from there over the whole island of Ireland, the swan singing as my father sang beautiful arias I always believed were of his own composing, and he was more than happy to let me think so.

I have circled round the moon, he would unleash his song, I have given her my heart, and I beg her to accept that humble gift. But Papa, I heard myself asking in my dream, how can you – how can anyone live without a heart? And he had no answer, putting all his strength into this most miraculous flight, his son on his downy back.

Then I'd wake, still happy, in his arms. He would kiss me

on my forehead, and say, breakfast. I'm going to eat you for breakfast. No, Papa, I would happily squeal, don't eat me. I am a cat, he would pretend, a great hairy cat, and you are a mouse, squeal if you are a mouse. So I squealed, and he said, I hear you, little mouse, now I must catch you. No, Papa, don't catch me, I giggled as he rolled me in his arms, I will make my granny give you breakfast, then you won't be hungry anymore.

What will she feed me? He wanted the list. Porridge and milk, sugar and butter, duck eggs and bacon, bursting sausages, puddings of all shades and shapes, strong tea. And coffee? he asked, any coffee? Not in this part of the world, stranger, I'd repeat in my Galway voice, sounding like Mama, making him content that I remembered to include her in our game.

I walk about the graveyard in whose Swiss clay he will soon be lying, far from his own dead. He will be lonely for sure. And what is it – the first stirring of grief? – but again I feel the wind swiped out of my sails as I retch with the shock, all air in this spot is sucked out of me. Maybe it is me dying, not Papa. And I recall how strange things happen, certainly in Galway. That same visit – or was it when my mother came with us? – we heard the story of a servant girl whose mistress treated the lass so harshly she drank bleach and died, choking, cursing the cruel lady of the house.

Granny sang a lament for the poor child, bringing tears to my father's eyes, but an aunt of Mama's stepped in and put a stop to this maudlin come-all-ye, by observing she knew this yarn, and its ins and outs, from a very different angle. Then tell all you know, my granny demanded.

Don't break your heart for this hussy, who went by the name of Maisie Sheehy, the aunt reported, and she was known to have led two young men sufficiently astray they left the Church and were struck down with tuberculosis as a reward for their negligence of Easter duty. Not once for the allowed time span to receive the host – the best part of four months surely – did they set foot at the altar rails. Well, they themselves, the pair of yahoos, they died roaring for the priest, as she did, the bold Maisie, whose red hair was her pride and joy, her crowning glory. She did not take her life deliberately, for it was not bleach she thought she was swigging, but the best of Limerick poitín, than which there is none finer, as a lady experienced in the consumption of strange liquids such as Miss Sheehy would know, she who could not so much drink the country as the continent – nay, the very cosmos itself – dry.

So when she thought – the man killer, that was the name we put on her and well deserved it was – when she thought she had a dose of the queer stuff in the bottle before her, didn't she down it in one go and died on the spot, fire erupting out of her every orifice. They said she smelt of sulphur emanating even from her grave.

My mother thought this story, even for her aunt, was a bit too far-fetched. She dared to question was it true in all parts? As true as you're sitting there, she was assured. And, the aunt continued, how do I know that? Because she is a relation of ours, you and myself, God forgive the two of us speaking ill of the woman, though she be frying in hell. We said nothing against her, my grandmother declared.

No, but you sat there and listened to me, and you never spoke in her defence, the aunt attacked, and that's as bad as accusing her. There was a song written about that story, and if you know it, I hope to Jesus you'll keep your mouths shut and not sing it, for they say it has the power to raise the dead, and I have no wish to come across anyone connected to these goings-on, I've bother of my own with corns crippling me.

What song might raise my father from his grave? Mama said she loved him for many reasons, but his voice was the greatest – that much she would admit now and forever. In Zurich, hearing German everywhere, I wonder in this year of Our Lord 1941 what crimes are committed in that language, and I soon cease from wondering, for to list the present iniquities of these sorry times, even in the innocent safety of Switzerland, I can hear my very blood itself congeal within my veins. Fear. Father had his favourite arias from Italian opera. His taste there was to be expected. Nothing too untoward would startle his listeners. While Mama loved to hear such pleasant melodies, but there was in German one song that touched her most acutely, and it was by the Austrian, Franz Schubert. Papa would sing it, and she would bend her head, her sober head I should add, for this tune had the power to still her and let her weep for all her dead.

Auf einen Totenacker
Hat mich mein Weg gebracht;
Allhier will ich einkehren,
Hab'ich bei mir gedacht.

And as he sang, she would sway her body to his music.

To a corphouse
I'll trek my way.
Here I'll settle,
I thought to myself.

He never chided her. Though he had little patience with her interruptions to his performance, on these occasions he would let her whispers translate.

Ihr grünen Totenkränze
Könnt wohl die Zeichen sein,
Die müde Wand'rer laden
Ins kühle Wirtshaus ein.

She let him finish that verse, and he politely waited as she lilted lowly to herself.

Tenebrous wreathes, dying, green
A sign we are sent for?

We who have wandered wearily,
Spent, exhausted, at this inn.

And though her music bore next to no relation to what
had poured from his mouth, though she had little notion
how the German fixed itself in its own patterns, still he let
her heart crack, remembering whatever it was she did from
the sorrows of her life.

Sind denn in diesem Hause
Die Kammern all' besetzt?
Bin matt zum Neidersinken
Bin tödlich schwer verletzt.

And here it was he might expect she would stop, too
damaged to draw breath, let alone speak, for when she
could, that was all she'd do – speak, and he'd listen to her
sore heart, repeating after each line, my father, my mother.

Then is this house entirely full?
My father, my mother?

Are all the rooms taken?
My father, my mother?

My body's ready to expire.
My father, my mother.

Death has quite destroyed me.
My father, my mother.

She would repeat the last line, adding only the words my father, my mother, your death has quite destroyed me. This was when my father would take my mother's hand, and it was as if they breathed as one till he finished – what was it? A lullaby to bring his troubled wife peace?

O unbarmherz'ge Schenke,
Doch weisest du mich ab?
Nun weiter denn, nur weiter,
Mein treuer Wanderstab!

He knew that she would let him end in silence, for she understood only too well what these words promised. She would have stopped weeping too, and there they would sit until she would nod her head, ask him to sing that hateful ballad. I used rush from the room. As a grown man, I am deeply embarrassed to admit this, but such is the nature of our family, that if you have even the slightest acquaintance with our comings and goings, I expect to be believed when I declare that it is a true thing I am saying when I hear a piece of – what? How would I describe it? Serenade, no – shanty, definitely no – dirge? That is warmer. All I know is that since hearing this strange piece as a boy, it has the capacity to unman me. All the more so now as an adult, for it appears to have acquired the power of prophecy.

I once seriously disturbed a gathering at lunch on a Sunday afternoon by stamping my feet on the floor and shouting no, no, stop it, stop that song. It was not my difficult and demanding sister who was causing the scene. No, it was the boy, the quiet child, so silent and reclusive I might not be there in the company, never, unlike her, attracting attention to myself.

What is the matter with you, Archie? Mama looked genuinely worried. I shook my head but could not confess what troubled me, for there and then I collapsed into a convulsion of sobs, choking me, buried in my father's lap. These did not cease, and they were of sufficient violence that Mama – I heard her crying out to Father, Jesus, Dick, what ails him, is he having a fit, could it be epileptic or what?

A medical man in the company assured her this was not the case. That particular illness was his specialist area, and I was showing no signs that I had succumbed to the disease. I could see such a look of relief cover Papa's face that I knew I must be brave and stop this excessive display so his mind could be put to rest. When I was under control again, my father pressed me to tell what had brought about this outburst. That awful song – the Irish one about a merry-go-round, a fairground – it scares the life out of me, I confessed, and I am sorry I never admitted it to you before, but please, do not sing it.

–That's what caused this chaos, the words of 'She Moved Through the Fair', is that it? Papa asked.

– It is, I admitted, I hate them, for I can see ghosts when you sing them and I think you and Mama will die soon, if I listen to them.

– Well, he's your son all right, Papa smiled at Mama, you have him well trained to be as bad as yourself, feeling himself haunted on every occasion. Will you watch what you say in front of the boy?

– The child can't help his own history, and don't you deny, my good man, that on your side of his house there's a more than passing acquaintance with those long dead and buried, she challenged him. The only thing would truly trouble me in this business is how early it's manifested itself. Not that it should shock me. That song has always and ever been considered unlucky.

– The first time I ever heard tell of that, he admitted.

– Then you should listen, she advised him.

– And what would I hear? Tell me, he demanded. When is it unlucky to sing–

– At a wedding, to sing it at a wedding, how do you not guess that even? Mama laughed at him. It can mean the married couple have no hope of lasting together.

– He's not at a wedding, is he? Papa observed, and he's hardly likely at his age to be taking a wife.

– That's exactly what worries me, she admitted, he's young to be sensing something not right in what he hears.

This was when Father burst into song.

The people were saying no two were e'er wed,
But one had a sorrow that never was said,
And she walked away from me with one star awake,
Like a swan in the evening moves over the lake.

Is that what put the wolves howling at your door, my son? The swan, does it frighten you? Or could it be the star? he wanted to know. Sure they're lovely and bright, stars and swans, aren't they? Might it be the sorrow that never was said?

Will you desist from teasing the boy? Mama warned him. Look, he's already going to bawl again.

So is it the sorrow – the sorrow never said? And what is that sorrow? Or maybe who is it would be more accurate? Could it be your sister?

Now you're drunk, Mama threatened him, you're very drunk, and you're stepping well over the line that's allowed in my kitchen. Don't you see how you're disturbing the child?

That's when he'd wrap me in his arms, humming the scary song to himself, caressing my hair, kissing my head, telling me there was nothing in this world to fear, though

I kept seeing ghosts as he murmured,

> Last night, she came to me, my dead love crept in,
> She crept in so softly, her feet made no din.
> As she moved away from me, these words she did say,
> It will not be long, love, till our wedding day –
> It will not be long, love, till our wedding day.

On my own wedding day I kept listening to that air, though no one played or sang it. I wondered did anyone else hear it haunt the feast, or was I alone the guilty party inviting disaster on the union? At one point I looked at my mother who was looking at my bride, and I saw no malice on either expression.

That day my father kept his distance from the whole company, as if he would not know any of us had he the choice. What have I done to offend the man? my own wife wondered. I had begun to notice how she was always wondering that, always thinking she had affronted someone and now they were paying her back, no matter how much I tried to convince her this was not so.

I hoped no ill omens would befall us, and I was relieved

we all seemed to be on our best behaviour. All proceeded swimmingly, despite my misgivings, until I heard out of the blue my sister shriek – Look, look up at the sky, that bird, is it an albatross?

Someone shut that stupid bitch up, my mother hissed, what is she trying to show off about now? That she knows this marriage won't last? We all know that, fuck her, including the happy couple, don't you?

Mama turned to us and asked, You're well aware this cannot last?

We did not contradict her, for it didn't last, she was correct in that then, and if she took pleasure from our misfortune, wasn't that her nature?

CHAPTER TWO

Wife

Bertha

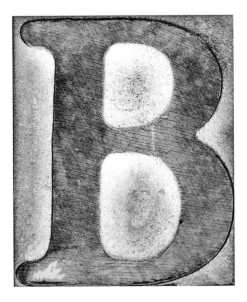

Galway, Ireland

Am I not the black pity of a woman? How often did I hear my own mother chant that refrain? She then would add that the cause of all grief in her life was her reluctance to become a nun, and if she had a chance to relive the days of her existence, then that's the path she would have followed – to the convent, best of food, best of accommodation, work about the house all done for you as you prayed the knees off yourself, and what was best of all? No men. Absolutely no men to bother you or to need minding. Who could not be happy – delirious even – with such a set up?

But what about us, Mama? What would have become of your children? If you'd become a nun, where would we be? In heaven, she said, annoying the hell out of the angels and the saints, as you annoy me on earth.

Wasn't that an appalling answer for her to give an innocent child? Is it a wonder I feel wanted nowhere? I suppose if you took things easy, and to my credit, I always try to do so, my mother's words made me allergic to promises of plenty in the next world, and I'd fiercely refuse to countenance any palaver about what's in store for us, if we believe in such nonsense as divine reward. That's what I told himself, my fellow, for it's what he wanted to hear.

If I have a fault, and I have many I admit, it's that this was what I'd always do. Tell him what pleased him. What was the point denying him? He'd get his way in the end. Of course, he would argue the opposite. He would describe me as a woman hell bent on leaving him heart-scalded by what I would or, more likely, would not do. Odd that two people living in such closeness should have exactly the opposite notion of how they tick. Or is it odd? Maybe we each of us develop a knack for not listening to what the other is saying. That's why, years ago, when he declared he was going to learn to lip-read, I told him it was the best thing he could ever do, so go on, full steam ahead. Did it ever go further than a declaration?

I can't ask him now, for he's lying there, his lips sealed. Nothing could shift a response from between them. Lips that once opened and out of them poured the sweetest of melodies, softest of sighs. There were times after he sang I swear his breath smelt like a woman's perfume – comical that, for he had the purest tenor voice ever put into a man's mouth. Say what you like, and I could say plenty, there was an occupation he did to perfection. An awful pity he didn't just stick to the music and leave the writing to other boyos who could do nothing but the one thing, and then never as well as him either – hence, his determination never to let it go.

Would he have been a happier man if he'd done so? Me a happier woman? What is happiness, any road? There was a beggar woman used call to my grandmother's house, regular as a clockwork mouse, twice a month in winter, once in summer, always on a Friday, looking for a feed of fish, but never mackerel. Though the poor creature be starving, she would not touch its flesh, maintaining it was what she called to our delight as children a lascivious beast whose behaviour disgraced the ocean. Behind her back we used mock her fancy way of describing a stupid old mackerel, and one day when I was older, I had to inquire from her why did she shun only this species.

What was I expecting to hear from her? A dirty story from under the seas? I was never a girl for such yarns at the best of times, so I doubt if it was that which prompted me. She told me I could never learn young enough the dire effect mackerel had on a young lassie. Eat your fill and more of it, and you would turn into the most beautiful girl ever to be seen in Connaught. Well may you jump hearing this as I can see you doing, she noticed, but pay full heed to what else I'm warning. Once you get a taste for this magic, it's like a man who gets a taste for red-haired hussies, there's no hope. Nothing else will satisfy. Isn't that what happened me? Isn't it why I lost house and home, family and friends – all in pursuit of becoming the loveliest of them all? Didn't I get what I wanted, and my face, wasn't there symphony after symphony, sonata after sonata, composed in my honour?

I never heard any, I remarked.

You wouldn't, she confirmed. What happened to them? I asked her, for some reason expecting her to lie – why I cannot say – but no, she told me truthfully, they were all forgotten, not a soul remembers a single piece, except herself. And did I know why?

I didn't – tell me.

Because she it was who wrote them, all in praise of her own splendour. She paid the price for this sin of pride. No one could recall a single note, and when she'd tried to remind them of the melodies she had plucked from the ether, what did the music provoke from this shower of begrudgers but a jeer, a thousand jeers, ringing in her ears, and all of them singing the same nonsense, you stole that from better fiddlers than yourself, you're claiming credit for another's labour.

The more she tried to deny this, the more she'd correct them, being well able to give chapter and verse exactly when she and she alone had been the hand that plucked these chords from nowhere, the more she was scorned by all and sundry, until once in the heat of argument a fat woman slapped her across the face with a mackerel that the beggar swore smiled at her tauntingly, daring her to blame an innocent fish for her lies and deceptions and all the bad cess that had brought her to this lowly status where she now found herself.

I listened and believed her. Then she asked had I the price of a night's lodgings?

How could I as a child have such a sum of money on me? Then ask the lady of the house, she urged. But I knew my grandmother's answer to that. It was the answer she gave to most requests. We are poor people, she would inform whoever asked for anything. We are poor people. These are the words I hate most in the English language, and when I told that to himself – was it in Dublin I first confessed this? If it was, then you would have heard him laughing in Galway.

Why did he think it so amusing? Why was he mocking me? Was it, I said, because he thought himself better than me and mine? Didn't he spring from the loins of an old windbag that couldn't leave that walking waif of his mother alone for the space of time to let her draw breath before she was up the pole with another babby? What right have you, I roared at him, what right have you to upcast my want when you are no better your good self?

I have no right, he said, that was why I was laughing. He left it at that, and I let him.

Others might have been tempted to regard what he said as no more than a back-answer you'd expect from a maid standing up to the housekeeper in a cheap hotel that would fleece you as soon as look at you, but I have enough gumption to admit when I'm wrong, and while wrong might not be the way to describe how I reacted to what he said, still and all I felt his honesty, when it came down to it, that we were, me and him, cut from the same cloth, and we'd never forget it.

Does he forget it now, lying there, near lifeless? How could I waken him? Will I tell him I'm going to pray for him? Would the shock of that stun him into saying something?

We were taught all the prayers in our school in Galway. My favourite was to Our Blessed Lady, the 'Memorare'. I did believe once upon a time very long ago that if I recited it, I would be heard and given everything I wanted, so I was careful, very careful not to be a greedy gut and look for too much. It would not do, I knew, to expect the heavens to open and douse me with divine blessings – not with clothes or shoes or a big sofa.

What was it I tried to cajole then out of Mary, Queen of Heaven? Days off school likely, forget sweets and toys, I accepted such favours were of the wrong sort and I should be ashamed to torment her looking to receive these childish pleasures. No, I had drummed it into my head that when you put the poor mouth on with the purpose of the Virgin listening to your needs and wants, then it should concern itself – the prayer – with health or the necessity to find a job or pass an exam.

Not that this lady talking here concerned herself too avidly with the examinations, as my mother used delight to remark, but she was one who shouldn't pass comments. My grandmother always said of her daughter, that lassie, she could not spell shite without a Q. Christ, was Ma livid when that was brought back into the conversation long after she believed it dead and buried. No, some cousin in her wandering mind or else a crone of a neighbour – there was one nicknamed Joan the Crone – they would bring it back again into circulation and there she was marked out for slander once more, if slander be the same as the truth.

And I did believe in the truth of that prayer. Long after I let all faith in so much of what had been nailed into us as God's tenets cease to trouble me in the very slightest, it would come back in the dark night and console me, even if I might be too young at the time to need much consolation. Jesus, I suppose you're never too young not to need that – even the infant in the cradle. I'm told when I was in the crib, I took to the holy water like a Wexford whore to whiskey, so all the more surprising I was not what they used to describe in Galway as gospel greedy.

Funny thing about that town, the way it divided its

people into those who would not stray outside their front door without a scapular round their neck or row of medals reputedly blessed by a cardinal or bishop on their Confirmation day, and the others who would not give the same bishop or cardinal the wind of their fart in honoured greeting. As always with my crowd, nobody knew who was what, so you could rely on someone being offended and slamming the front door shut in a fit of pique, vowing never to address another word to that shower of infidels or holy Joes. You wouldn't know if you were coming or going having a conversation, should the subject of religion arise.

Best then say nothing, but can you imagine the likes of us holding our tongues?

Speaking of Confirmation, we all chose another name, and I took Felicity, largely to annoy that grandmother I mentioned in relation to my own mother's lack of learning. The same woman could provide you with all the songs ever heard through the confines of the city and the wilds of County Galway, but was not so hot when it came to putting pen to paper. They were united in wonder and a bit of disgust at the choice of Felicity. How in under good Christ did you come up with that gander of a name – is it a saint's?

Will you be allowed to use it?

That was their response when I let slip they would have to dig me into the grave before I'd pick Bernadette, as they both were urging.

Bernadette's a lovely name, they insisted, what do you find wrong with it? Because it sounds like a sheep. I'm sure she did mind sheep in her day, I was informed, there's nothing untoward with that at all – wasn't she singled out for special honour at Lourdes and her a poor country girl like yourself? Then it's hardly likely to happen twice, is it, I maintained, I'm not going to see any visions and even if I were, I'd stick to Felicity. Do as you please, do as you always do, my mother nodded to her mother, expecting and finding agreement. I'll never get my tongue round it, she insisted. Who do we know called that? Nobody, I assured her. What was she? A martyr, I informed them.

Why don't you go the whole hog and call yourself Robert Emmet, they asked, now there was a martyr, a man who died for Ireland, would your Felicity have done like-wise? She was a martyr in Rome for the Christian faith, I informed them, if you read your prayer book you'd know that. The age of that one, advising me to read my missal, you have some cheek, my lady. I'd slap the badness out of her if I didn't think she'd hit me back, my mother chuckled, an old saying and a true saying, you have them as you reared them, I've made the stick to beat my back. You said it, my grandmother noted, so how did they martyr poor Felicity?

Saint Felicity, I corrected her, give her the proper title, for she earned it considering how she died. That's what I'm asking, how did she go? Grandmother repeated. I had no more notion than the man in the moon what way the poor bitch popped her clogs, so I had better find something they'd believe. Was it by fire? Granny wondered, or did they knife her? Maybe they flayed the skin from her and fed her bones to the dogs? They had a great fondness for that class of activity in Rome back then. How would you know? my mother demanded. The same thing happened to a woman in Moycullen, well before you were born, my granny said, the husband was the culprit, he got away with it though. How? He ate the evidence, he ate what was left of her, his poor wife. Wouldn't it make you think twice about marrying? Though such advice is a bit late in the day for us, she observed.

Nothing like that happened to Saint Felicity, I said, she

did not die by any of the methods you mentioned. They set fire to her, and she was consumed by flames. Just like Joan of Arc. In fact as a homage to her and maybe as an omen of what was to become her destiny, the same Joan took Felicity as her Confirmation name, also much against her parents' wishes.

Weren't they right? my mother sneered, didn't she too go up in flames? I have only one thing to say about all this, my granny added, for I'm thinking of that poor girl, whatever you call her, and the sore end she came to, being eaten alive by the blazes of hell, and her a good-living, decent being – why in the midst of all this horror, why in such peril, why when all hope was lost, did she not turn to the sweet mother of God? Why did she not know Mary would have protected her as she tried to protect her only beloved son? Why didn't that Roman girleen not say her 'Memorare'?

You see now how I was reared? You can understand why I'd turn in that direction? How such recourse was ingrained through me? Himself thinks he knows it all about me and mine, but he wouldn't credit the half of it. How could he, when I haven't told him? That's my look-out, but if I were to wonder why I kept my secrets – as many as I did – what would I answer? What would be my defence?

That he could never, ever keep anything to himself. The man even told his son how he was born. If the boy's head were not turned by knowing such things about his mother, who would wonder at it? When the child looked, what could he not see but that same mother naked, swimming with blood? That planted firmly in his poor brain – how could the boy not have the most confused ideas about women?

I'd be the first to admit that I was the one who said my son married an invisible woman – I swear to Jesus that she was just not there. It was not so much a question of what he saw in her as of what he saw at all? Did she exist? Well, she must have, for they signed the contract legally uniting them, but the bitch was anaemic to the extent that I doubt if there was a drop of blood in her veins. Was there a vein even in her body? Was there an ounce of solid flesh to be found in her? At the end it's said she did a runner back to her own people, but would they have noticed her returning?

I doubt it.

And of course the finger of blame for the ruination of my son's happiness was pointed in his mother's direction.

I'll pay it no heed. What crime am I guilty of? Have I not always tried to do the best for me and mine, and what thanks were ever offered? The mockery of himself. I could hear the sneering if I were to admit to the divine goodness I turned to for succour and mercy when there was neither in the vicinity of my home as we wandered through whatever city of Europe where he might find the few shillings to keep me in drawers and himself in drink and a bite in the mouth of our bonhams. That, to the likes of you, is a suckling pig. An uncle from Sligo passed on its usage, and it's always been fondly employed by our ones. Himself though, my one and only, he would not be too fond if he knew whose blessing I craved on the whole shower of us. Or maybe he would, contrary fucker as he was, and me his match, I admit.

I look at him lying helpless on this bed in the lonely city where we've ended up on the run from the bastards who'd eat us without salt should we stumble into them. What makes people hate? It must be the roughest thing in the world to live with a heart so hardened that it can't hear another being weeping in pain. Dear Christ, let no one say that about me after I'm dead and buried. Let me receive a softer word as a woman. I tried my best to harm nobody. That dying man, he is my witness. He would back me up in that claim. And what am I doing talking about death being so near? Am I hastening it on its way to him? And why do I hesitate to say the words of the prayer that never failed me, or if it did I've forgotten when? Is it just because I fear he'd laugh at me and jeer?

No, it can't be, for I'd give anything even for him to deride me – to have even that much life in him. Then what is halting me?

I don't know. Maybe I don't want to. Just say it and be done.

Who knows what reaction it will provoke? Might get a rise out of him. One time everything did. Not today or yesterday. Still, I'm one to talk. You could now parade a whole naked hurling team in front of me and I wouldn't thank you. I'm talking serious. I wouldn't know now what to do with a bare cock. Smoke it maybe. Get a bit of satisfaction that way if no other. I'll be struck down for that kind of chat and me intending to invoke the Blessed Virgin.

What kind of woman was she at all, I wonder? From what little I know, I'd say she was fierce for the cleaning.

Likely never had a scrubbing brush out of her hand. The talk of Nazareth for being house proud. Had she St Joseph and Jesus in a state if they dirtied a clean shirt she'd spent hours scrubbing? Worn the knees off herself polishing.

A neighbour of ours, Mrs Rooney, was notorious for leaving her kitchen floor slippery as ice. When queried why, she said she lived in hope her husband's mother might visit. There was a chance the old witch might break her neck if she slipped, for she showed little other sign of ceasing to torment those afflicted by any connection to her. The Rooneys were widely regarded as not being right in the head, although I was pally with the eldest girl, Suzie. Poor Suzie – she took to the drink badly, and the last I heard was walking the streets of Cardiff, if you please, whatever notion took her there.

I wonder did she pray as I'm about to? A fine-looking youngster, gorgeous hair, thick, jet black. The old lady they all hated, she threatened to put a stop to her gallivanting, as courting was sometimes called in those distant days. She waited for Suzie to come home one night. Now it was late, after two in the morning. That must be acknowledged. She had two big thick sons of hers in attendance – boys you wouldn't dare look crooked at in case they'd break your mouth for having the monstrous cheek to set eyes on them. One of them intended to wear a knuckleduster but the other persuaded him not to. Far too rough a punishment surely to use against a girl. There was no necessity for any other instrument than a pair of shears. They could work vengeance as well as any weapon or boot against a woman. They lay in wait for her, hiding inside the gateway of an abandoned forge.

She – the old one – got the men to grab Suzie when she ventured past and hold her against a wall. She hacked the girl's beautiful hair off so you could see her scalp. If they expected the youngster to cry out of shame and beg their mercy, they had the wrong soldier. She didn't even blink an eye – just kept looking straight ahead of her, saying nothing. That defiance must have been infuriating. Didn't the old bitch skelp Suzie across the face? See how many of your fancy men like the look of you now, the witch jeered, hoping to provoke at least a tear out of the girl.

Suzie didn't oblige. Not so much as a sob left her lips. She kept her eyes bored into her tormentor, ignoring the guffaws of the two centurions attending the scene. Finally she spoke, and word has it this is what she declared: Did you enjoy inflicting on me what you've just done? I hope you have, for it will be the last time you raise your hands against me in any shape or form. Remember that the next time you're seen beating the breast of yourself at the altar rails. Remember what I'm about to deliver you.

And with that didn't Suzie start to say the 'Memorare', much to the consternation of the three who assaulted her.

– Remember, O most gracious Virgin Mary–

– Why are you invoking the name of Mary, stop it at once, you heathen, her grandmother demanded, to no avail.

– That never was it known–

– Will you stop this blaspheming, what are you trying to do? The old one was now panicking.

– That anyone who fled to thy protection–

– Stop it, Suzie, the grandmother warned.

– Implored thy help–

– You know what bad luck will follow this.

– Or sought thine intercession was left unaided.

– Make her shut her lying mouth, the older and more frightened of the bullies pleaded.

– Inspired by this confidence–

– Our Lady is listening to all of this, the old woman threatened.

– Jesus, I hope she's not, the other bruiser stuck his oar in.

– I fly unto thee–

– What are you going to ask for anyway? they questioned her.

– O Virgin of virgins, my mother–

– I'm sure the same virgin is having a good laugh listening to that whore try to defile something so holy as this prayer, the younger bucko said.

– To thee do I come, before thee I stand–

– She has no shame, her grandmother observed.

– Sinful and sorrowful.

– Sinful for certain, but I'd not be too sure about the sorrow, would you be, boys? she asked.

– O Mother of the Word Incarnate–

– I've often wondered what in hell that all means, how can you mother a word? the younger lad wondered.

– It's a mystery, just believe it, the grandmother menaced him.

– Despise not my petitions–

– Will you enlighten us what they may be? she was asked.

– But in thy mercy hear–

–You will not be heard, rest assured of that.

– And answer me.

They let Suzie finish her prayers. She did not give them time to plague her further. Rather she eyeballed them and said out straight, in case you want to learn what I want, it is that all of you, from the oldest to the youngest, die roaring and it is within my earshot. I would not so much as offer you a sip of water to ease your suffering. Know this much – you are hated from this hour onward. I have no time nor respect for you. You are the dirt beneath my feet.

So that's the thanks I get at the end of my days, the granny was near crying, that's all I need expect, well, you've shown me your true colours, I should have seen them years ago. Don't darken my door again – you'll never cross under my roof. If you act like a tinker and talk like one, you can live like one. Never come back.

I have no intention of ever doing so, Suzie assured her. I won't wait for tomorrow. I'll go this night. You'll never set eyes on me again, nor will any in Galway.

And we never did. Not a sign of our pal.

You'd hear things in passing – hence the story about her

in Cardiff from an Oranmore man who'd been working in Wales down the pits, but who knows, was it her at all he'd glimpsed? I always thought that our paths would cross, especially when I was working in that hotel in Dublin. She might call asking for me. But no, no. It never happened. Still, I thought of her often, especially at the end of October. That might have been her birthday, I'm not sure, but I am certain the two of us loved that part of the year when it would soon be Hallowe'en. How long since I celebrated that feast day? All Souls, 31 October, All Saints, 1 November. My family always threw a big party, the envy of Galway.

Hard to believe but nuts – nuts were a novelty then. Lovely in their strange shells. Hazels, Brazils, monkeys, almonds, walnuts – smelling of cats for some reason, the last ones I mentioned. In Paris you could buy them all the year round in any shop you'd enter. I made a show of us at one swanky dinner when come the meal's end, they displayed the nuts and I asked, was it Hallowe'en or what? Sure those big noises – well, they thought they were – never heard in France of such a date, and I was given a look by himself that I'd better not start trying to explain. For once I did as he demanded, because that was the occasion when Suzie appeared in my mind's eye, devouring slices of barmbrack, and all I could do was watch her eat.

Would it be fair to say that Galway ones, we're always ravenous? Are we, to a man, woman and child, always shovelling grub down our gullets? Let me tell you, everywhere I travelled – Italy, France, Switzerland – they can wine and dine without restraint in all destinations. I say more power to them. Were himself now capable of a morsel or two, I'd be the first to take pleasure feeding him. Maybe a slice of roast chicken, or a wing, a taste of salty ham perfumed with sugar and cloves on the skin, a wedge of chocolate cake sandwiched with apricot jam or a hefty slab of bread drowning in the best Irish butter, if you can get your hands on it off someone travelling from home. He'd relish the lot of that, make no mistake, and I'd be the happy woman to see him sated. I wonder did I ever pass on to him that expression of my grandfather's – he would claim that, at the end of his days, he could lift nothing heavier than a knife and fork nor raise only a glass. I must not have, for he would have repeated it to me to check he had his wording of it accurate, and I cannot recall that ever happening.

I recall my grandfather though – that man was a fount of knowledge about Hallowe'en. He was strong as an ox, able to break nuts just by squeezing them in his palms. Sometimes he'd do funny voices, pretending to be the shell squeaking as it broke, squealing in a high shriek not to be torn apart. As children we loved this performance, watching him like hawks, listening to his jokes, begging him to do it again, again, again. Then he'd stop and tell us to enjoy our party. We did because the bowls full of fruit, the baskets crammed with sweets – that would be a rare enough sight. We each had our two apples and an orange, a chocolate bar and a sherbet lollipop, four slabs of toffees and a bottle of lemonade. Paradise.

Some of us saved bits and pieces to eat later on or the following day. Not me. I wolfed the lot, for I wanted to be out and about on the night that was in it, playing games of chasing.

Were you chasing ghosts, or were they chasing you?

Who said that? Jesus Christ, who spoke just then? Was is you, Dick? Richard, now don't do this to me – did you speak to me? Or am I only imagining things? My mother said that might prove to be the bane of my life, having a lively imagination. Or being a liar, depending on who was describing me.

I did hear his voice just now, didn't I? It was him asking me about ghosts, wasn't it? What did I say or do to rouse him? Was it just by referring to the night itself? Did the mere mention of Hallowe'en shake him out of his stupor, if only for a sentence? Should I answer his questions?

The answer is, I don't know who was doing the chasing. We walked about in gangs, doing some innocent badness. One year, myself and the same Suzie, we overstepped the mark with our games, and we knew we had. Half, if not the entire population of Galway is what we describe as being bad with the nerves. This can account for everything from not washing your windows to murdering your husband with a stout blackthorn stick, flattening his skull like a pancake, claiming it wasn't him you were putting the kibosh on but a replica the fairies had left in his stead. The wife who tried that as an alibi got twenty years. When she got out, she still claimed it was worth it. Anyway, there was a neighbour, a Sam McGowan, who suffered badly from the shakes – though he never touched a drop – when the darkness descended on him, and the night he and his own dreaded most was Hallowe'en.

Well, he had it planted in his head that there was among the McGowans a belief that a loud knock at the door was a terrible sign and that this had been historically proven. If it had been, then it was news to all belonging to him, but none could dissuade him. The poor fellow believed with all his heart, this knock was unlucky. Now what do you think was the consequence of this? All children love a bit of mischief, and who could resist at Hallowe'en the old habit of banging on a neighbour's door and then running away like the hammers of hell before they opened it? Harmless enough, you would say, but not so if the man you're tormenting thinks it's the banshee dropping by with a Mass card for the soul of the departed and it's his name she's signed on the bottom.

The upshot of all this was, of course, there was a queue of us lining up to persecute Sam. Why didn't he just leave his door open and catch the culprits? Well, he lived with his mother who was crippled with a bad chest, and Galway at the end of October is no Riviera. You daren't leave a window ajar unless you plan to entertain a dose of pneumonia.

So, Sam was ripe for the mocking. But this year it

was rumoured he could take no more taunting. Maybe tonight he might not relent from getting the police – maybe you would be behind bars at his insistence. That was the risk you undertook should you try to get a laugh or a chase out of him.

We'd better try nothing, Suzie cautioned, leave him this year. I was shocked at her. Since when had she turned into such a yellow belly? It was always me being the cowardy custard. But not this time. I said if she wouldn't knock at McGowans' door, then I would. You do, she challenged, and you best be ready to run like a scalded cat, and if you don't, I'll tell everyone. Better to be laughed at than to dirty yourself out of fear, and I could tell from the jumping in my stomach there was a strong chance of that happening. I decided it best I get a quick move on. No use hanging about trying to hear if he's pacing inside, waiting to leap immediately on whoever dares this night to disturb whatever peace the poor man could ever summon for himself.

I ran to the house, and then, shocking myself as much as anything or anyone else, it wasn't a knock I gave but raising my brogue, I kicked the lining out of the wood.

The sheer force of it must have stopped him stone dead,

for the door didn't spring open and I had a bit of time to dash, followed by Suzie, who was laughing herself to death. We heard him deliver a mouthful of oaths after us, with his old mother telling him calm down – Sam, calm down, they're not worth following, leave them be, son. I don't know for sure if he took her advice for we were too blinded by fear to look back and see was he on our trail. Suzie and her people knew the warren of streets in all arts and parts of the city like the back of their hand, so I trooped after her, happy to let her lead me through highways and byways and nooks and crannies of Galway, for we met, thanks be to Christ, no one who would know us, and I sincerely hoped Suzie would be able to find her way home.

We'd been warned all our lives about the river and the quays and beware of ships and sailors, never listen to them. Here now was where we found ourselves. If I'd thought about the danger I would have been petrified, too scared to take a step, yet I knew it was most urgent I keep my wits about me and be ready to race away should there be need to escape. We walked hand in hand, feeling we'd be safe if we stuck together. Nothing seemed untoward. The place was dark but quiet. We were feeling a little brave when we heard a voice ask us, what are you two girls looking for? You're wandering here at this hour of a Hallowe'en night, why?

We did not know the man who spoke, nor did he claim any acquaintance with us. I felt no lack of manners in telling Suzie under my breath not to speak to him. His accent sounded funny, foreign even, but then I realised where he was from. The Aran Islands. Wasn't the English language alien to them, so well versed in Gaelic, speaking nothing but that among themselves. We had an Aunt Rose on my father's side who'd married a fisherman from Inishmore, I think – and he took her to live there, never letting her back to the mainland. She claimed she didn't miss it, all you could want in life she had it where she lived, and her family believed her when she said that as she looked around her at the state of the world, she was the happiest of the whole lot of them. At one time her husband would call to us for his cup of tea when he'd come to the city, but that stopped. It was believed some offence was taken, but he would not reveal what and nobody wanted to know. He is reputed to have told his relations in Dominic Street that he believed we binned every cup he drank out of whenever he'd walked from our door. Does that buck eejit think I have money to burn, my mother asked, to throw away china just because his lips touched it? Let him go to hell and no longer bother me. His wife's as odd as two left feet, and so is he. Well matched, the pair of lunatics.

And it was his voice I could hear in the stranger now speaking to us, wondering what we were doing here. He repeated the question and this time before I could stop her, Suzie replied, we're minding our own business, and so should you be. Bold as brass that one, when she wanted to be. Aren't you the courageous girl, he retorted, hasn't that put me in my place? We don't care where your place might be, though we can make a guess, I added, just leave us alone. Another smart colleen, where would you guess my place is? he challenged. We don't have to answer any of your questions, Suzie reminded him, now will you be so good as to allow us make our way to home? Such politeness, the island man complimented her, haven't you the dainty tongue in your head?

She has a dainty toe in her boot, as have I, I warned him, take care it's not firmly planted up your hole.

Would you credit, what he next tried to palm off on

us? He said to us that if we were to give him even the inkling of a court, it could well be the last one he'd ever enjoy, so would we not soften our hearts and let him have a hint of a feel? I looked at Suzie, who was looking at him saying nothing, but I came out with, Well now, Mister, you're scraping the barrel and no mistaking, have you not the slightest dreg of shame?

What shame is it for a dying man to implore? What shame in pitching for a last favour before kicking the bucket? Have either of you a heart inside you at all? he wanted to know.

Indeed I've a heart, I let him know, and a hard one it is after hearing every sob story could be thrown in a body's face, listening to the lies of Ireland pouring out of a prize chancer's mouth. Your very teeth are turning green with shame spinning such awful stories as you're now doing.

Is it for that reason I tell you I'm dying? he asked. Would you leave off with that nonsense, said I, you're as healthy as the next man. Then didn't Suzie pipe up, What has you on your last legs? Is it a sleeping sickness or the tuberculosis that's taken half, if not two-thirds, of the men of Ireland? His answer was not what either of us expected.

He had been placed under sentence of death by a creature

he'd met in the sea while fishing on his currach. You'll be telling me next it was a mermaid, I said, bursting out in a laugh, would you ever catch yourself on? Who'd fall for such nonsense? Was it a mermaid? Suzie wanted to know, and I swear she was in earnest asking. Would you like it to have been? he smiled at her so sweetly you'd think they were stepping out together. Was it a mermaid? she repeated.

Why are you so anxious to know this? he asked her out straight. Because I think that's what I am, she answered him. No, not a mermaid, he said calmly, there was nothing maid-enly about the creature who passed on to me that fatal news. Suzie asked, was it a bird then? Some white gull that singled you out to hear and understand what it was cawing? Aye, he agreed, it was a fowl of some order or other, and it flew straight into my lap and took its ease there, as tame as a dove – but that's not what it was, for how could a dove survive the wet and winds of the Aran Islands? Then what was its species? she wondered.

I can tell you that, it was a sand martin, he said, there in all its glory, the brown head and rump, its white belly and throat, smelling of the Sahara whence it might have just flown, for it was singing in a strange language that could have been Arabic or Aramaic, I can't say, I know neither, but I followed its refrain for there was no mistaking the rattle at the song's end, convincing me that, for the two of us, the game was up. Now, do you not regret you weren't beside me on my boat?

Your currach, I corrected him, but she, Suzie, had clammed up. After what seemed like an age, she asked the two of us, You won't tell anybody what I said, will you? They would kill me. Who would? I asked. My people, she said, for they're not my people. It's why they hate me. Why they're so cruel. They found me and took me from the Atlantic, and as I grow older, funny enough I remember more clearly now than closer to when it happened as I was hauled out of the waves, my mother wailing to them to give me back, but they left her to weep on the shore. It's said you could hear her crying there at night for years after, raging, searching for her lost little one.

How for the love of the crucified Christ, were you ever a mermaid? I observed, haven't you feet beneath you, and not the tail of a fish? I can explain that, she said. Then the floor is all yours, I invited her, away you go. It's all a question of belief about what you see, she declared, do you believe or not in mermaids? I do not, I told her honestly. Do you believe in them? she asked the island man. I do believe, he said. Then that precisely accounts for the difference, she insisted, you don't believe, and so you see feet. He does believe, so he sees the tail. He knows what I am, don't you? she said turning to him.

I don't, he shocked her. Why not? she demanded. Because you've told us, he informed her, and such a secret must be forever under lock and key until it's either taken to the grave with you, or you go back to the depths of the ocean. You've done neither, so I think you have just been lying through your teeth, trying to trick me, a poor fisherman. The pair of you, go back to your ma's fireside, warming your arses before you hit the hay, safe and snug in your own shakedowns.

Suzie looked at him as if he were lice. Then she opened her mouth and spoke very lowly. The sand martin spoke the truth, she said, you will die, it will be soon, and no creature from the sea or air will step in to save you when the currach sinks, as it now must. Am I to understand you are placing a curse on me? he wanted to know. Understand what you like, she snapped.

They say no curse is ever heard without it rebounding on

the one who spoke it, leaving her, who was without mercy enough to cast it, coming one day to look for the very same mercy she lacked, and being refused it. It's a smart woman knows this is a weapon to be used sparingly, if at all. When I think of Suzie and wherever she might be wandering at night, through what city, Cardiff or not, what streets, what docks, what piers, does she remember that uncanny conversation, and her believing she was what so obviously she wasn't, yet ready to argue otherwise till the cows should come home? Does she ever imagine what she said attacking that Aran man would affect all she's done to herself? What has she brought on her two shoulders, her and her alone? Isn't she the unfortunate?

And me – me, am I the same? No, I'd argue the opposite. I would say when push comes to shove, I'm doing all right. Maybe more than that even. Blessed, if you're inclined to look at things in such a light – and we're not, as a family. We would be united on that. We're united on most things. We have our ups and downs. But we stick together. Or we try to. I'd be the first to admit that not everything has been easy going. The struggle for money when we were starting, that was a rough station. Neither himself nor myself were the best at providing for rainy days, but my excuse is every day in Galway the heavens bucket down, what else would you expect? We held body and soul together best as we could. A few friends had to put their hands into their pockets and bail us out, that is very true, but they believed in his genius, as did I, and they gave us the necessary to survive at times. You pay a price for struggling, though. Some would declare the price we paid was our daughter.

A difficult girl, no denying. Her father's ruined her. His little darling. His pride and joy, he might declare. And I'm not afraid to admit the many ways she knows and always has known how to wrap him round her little finger, her smart ruses to snare him – she daren't try such machinations on me – they have me heartbroken at the way she could destroy the lot of us, if I were not up to her, for haven't I seen the like before? Is there a family in Galway that doesn't have one in it – usually a female – who could cut the legs from under you with their letting on they need special attention, when a good thrash on the fat arse might prove the most effective of all cures needed to calm them down. But of course, if you say that out straight, you're the worst in the world, so, against my nature, I keep quiet on the subject of that lassie, certainly in front of strangers.

Not that any vow of silence applies to the same young lady. There are tribes I hear tell out foreign in the darkest part of the earth where they tie some sort of handkerchief about the faces of girls to stop their finding fault with whatever is their lot. It's said they pull their teeth out to make sure that any speech is sore, very sore indeed and you'd think more than twice before you'd be so bold as to give your opinion on this, that or the other. There was a family not that far from us where the father bred the fear of God into all his youngsters, but especially his womenfolk, where they'd feel the weight of his hand across their mouths should they ever make a comment that could in any way be construed as contradicting him. Wouldn't I have been the smart woman if I'd followed suit with that most troublesome offspring rather than honouring her every whim? Of course I could only do as I was allowed, and for that I have to blame himself who would let her burn the house down if that was what she demanded.

I speak with some authority on that matter, having seen her in action with fire. To her a box of matches was some kind of plaything. Strike a match, set a curtain ablaze, watch the pretty shades melting. How many times did I stop her in time? How many times did I accordingly stop myself from letting the world know something was wrong – seriously wrong with what we were rearing under our roof? Why did I not brave her father's wrath when he'd roaringly dispute that any sign of weakness in the head could not happen where one of his was concerned? Eyes see what they want to, ears hear as they please, there's no persuading some, but at least I can spare myself the biggest of blame when it comes to pointing the finger at who should stand most accused for not facing up to the worst. I would have got none or next to no thanks had I said how much she was in need of treatment.

Will I ever forget the night she proved that to me beyond all reasonable doubt? We were in a nice restaurant, myself, himself, Archie, her and a long string of Protestant misery from County Dublin who claimed he had travelled to Paris devoted only to serving the great writer. I had my grievous doubts about the same boy's intentions, and while some maintained the opposite, it is my contention he saw she would grow crazy about him and would do Christ knows what for the sake of a quick court, so he led her up the garden path and all the way to Renvyle to keep in with the supreme artist who was her father. Her devotion to this chancer, it was pitiful to watch, and maybe I was not the most attentive of mothers and made sure matters ceased, but how could I diminish her attentions towards him when he was clearly the apple of her eye and every other organ she possessed and the only unalloyed joy she might ever have known?

He got a bit of a revelation about her that night. We all did, I suppose. It was a swanky enough place, but we were holding our heads high, watching carefully what we were drinking, and then the waiter came for the order. Didn't I make the mistake of letting the young princess precede her mother, she could decide first what food she might deign to eat. He asked her to repeat the dish requested, and she did. Magpie.

She wanted to start with a feed of magpies. Since the men had buried themselves in their menus, I was the one felt obliged to point out this would not be possible. The French are an ingenious people – certainly more than the Irish – at what they consider edible in flesh, fish and fowl, but not even they could make magpies a delicacy to consume.

She begged to differ. Why? her father asked. I ate them as
a child, she recalled. Where? her brother wanted to know. In
my mother's bed – she fed me the whole bird, beak, feathers, she told him, she made me eat it all. I wouldn't let her
away with this, pointing out to her that to the best of my
knowledge neither my good self nor any belonging to me
would have the slightest notion how to cook a magpie. You
baked them, she contradicted me. What? I challenged her,
how in hell did I bake them? In a pie, she explained, and it
cost sixpence. I follow her, her father said suddenly. Then
you do more than I do, I let him know, what is she talking
about? That's when the Protestant skeleton shook his bony
mouth and broke his customary silence.

Sing a song of sixpence,
A pocketful of rye,
Four and twenty blackbirds
Baked in a pie.
When the pie was opened,
The birds began to sing.
Wasn't that a dainty dish
To set before the king?

She clapped her hands like a child, as did her father, delighted for some reason or other. The waiter was standing looking at us as if we were cracked. He just wanted us to make up our minds. You will eat fish, I insisted, as I will, and less of this carry on. I was glaring in the direction of her father, I was ready to kill him for encouraging her in this silly carry on. She was having none of it. She insisted she would eat nothing if she could not dine on magpie, and she wanted it here and now. The waiter, to my shock, played along. He said he would check in the kitchen, did so and came back to announce there was a great shortage in Paris of that particular bird. Might he recommend quail?

The scream emitting from her mouth shocked us all. I thought Archie was going to weep with embarrassment, poor fellow. I decided it best not to dignify her rudeness with any censure whatsoever, but made it clear when I rose from my chair I had no intention of allowing this bitch dictate that we were to spend an evening doubled over with shame. She had another think coming if such public outrage could unsettle me. I saw my drunk father pull his drawers down and, like an animal, dirty the streets of Galway, his cock waving in the pink wind. Did she think I would do a runner from this carry on with my tail between my legs, disgraced by her? The next thing I saw was her grabbing a jug of water. She then poured it over her lap, drenching it, the blue of her dress blackening.

I let her father make the apology. Archie accompanied me to the door, fetching my coat, politely not hearing my guts rattle with the hunger, for not a bite of food could be eaten in this establishment after what we'd witnessed tonight. I doubt now if himself will be able to turn his back on what would soon be necessary to be done and no mistake. I took no pleasure in leaving him to handle this mess, but my point is it is largely of his making. And it's from his side this bad blood has flowed to her brain.

You can imagine how that would have gone down if I'd dared breathe a word along those lines. The same drunken father I've more than once mentioned, he would surely be hurled in my face. But his weakness was drink, pure and simple. And such simple associations cannot be made about my daughter. My daughter – it's odd how hard I find it to say that statement. Why should that be the case? There was no one about me to ask, and it was hardly the kind of thing I could put in a letter home to my own mother. Who might get their Galway claws on it and read the secret? But she would have said something to take the weight of my dislike for my girl from my shoulders. Was it dislike anyway? Were it so, it might have weakened. Melted with the years. But it didn't. Not in the slightest way. So I doubt if it could be put down to that. No, if I am to be forced into admitting what I believed lay at the root of what distanced us, I'd say fear.

How did I fear her? I can't describe it, because I never would admit that, though the world knows she gave me reason enough. One Christmas I tried to buy her affection. For her present she got the most expensive doll ever made, beautiful, moving eyes, tender lips, a blush like a cream rose on her cheek, her dress cut from crimson silk, and her tiny feet fitted in little boots of softest leather. Could you guess what she did to it? She sliced every stitch off its back, dismantled every limb, cut the shoes to bits.

It now might seem like a warning, but what way did I react to the sight of this massacre?

I burst out laughing. Not the wisest move, I admit, but I'm the kind who would see something comical in destruction, as if the child didn't give a tinker's curse what she did, and what would be made of it. Gratitude was out the window. She would not so much bite the hand that gave as draw blood from it. And me, I was with her on that score. Still, I should have curbed that side of myself and taken this business under control. I didn't.

Or maybe he should have, her father.

I've said he spoilt her, but that's not half the story. If you want proof, look how he treated Archie. The poor son barely got a notice there, from that quarter. It's why I always and ever took his side. Nobody else would. The great artist found fault with me on account of this, of course. He'd say, Women, what is it about you as a sex? You'd knife each other as soon as stand together – same with my sisters in Dublin. Either so docile they'd faint rather than bid you good morning, or they got stuck into each other, battling morning, noon or night, never knowing agreement.

I beg your pardon, I differed, such a state was never the story with me and my sisters. We were together through thick and thin. None could divide us. And that stretched to the whole clan of us. No one could stand in our way. We were unbreakable–

And you still think you are, he shot back at me, that's what has us as we are, you not willing to admit our daughter will be grand, if we give her time. How much time does her highness require, I asked, that she'll deign to have a civil or indeed sane conversation with her own people? You and her, you gang up against me constantly. Against Archie as well.

He tried to laugh me out of this, but I would not be swayed and I held my ground. He was intent on provoking me this time, for he would not let up, insisting again I devote to her the attention she's been craving since I was the unfortunate woman who gave birth to her, and her very cries then split my head open. So I went further than I'd ever dared before, and I said to him, Dick, I can hardly be held responsible for the way she's infected, that's all your doing.

There might have been a time I'd regret not holding my tongue rather than using the word infected, but to be honest this was now long past. I knew the consternation it might cause, but there's occasions it's best to do more than bite the bullet but catch it instead and make a four-course dinner out of it. He bided his time before he came back and asked would I kindly have the consideration to enlighten him what I meant by infected? I would not be so foolish as to give him the straight answer he was dying for me to deliver, so I pinned all the troubles between myself and her down to the way she addressed me. She's been reading you far too much, I suggested, I can make neither head nor tail of what the pair of you are on about, but it's turned her head entirely and don't you deny it.

He said indeed he would not deny it at all, but at least there was one in the house who understood him. Well, bully for the pair of you, I congratulated him, may you both be happy together, licking stamps for a living and sending begging letters to anyone fool enough to listen to your flotsam and jetsam. All our life we've been living on handouts.

I knew it, he knew I knew it, but I'd never thrown it so fiercely in his face before, and I was not sure how he'd take it.

Like a whirling dervish, that's how. Have I ever seen him that angry? I suppose I have, but you forget the bad times. That's why I now forget what it was he called me, but you can be sure it was not pleasant, nor did I refrain from giving as good as I got. It was when she coughed I noticed the cause of this warfare was standing listening to all, the door ajar, hearing the words, saying nothing. What's keeping you there? I called, come in and give us the benefit of your wisdom. After all, aren't we discussing what in Jesus to do with you?

That's when she told us not to worry about herself – she was going to get married. Let me guess, I humoured her for the time being, is the lucky groom by any chance Protestant – from a sound clerical family in County Dublin, frequenters of Trinity College, given to a mournful look, with a bad habit of sucking his teeth, and worshipping your father for his lonely genius? I hate to break this to you but in my opinion he'd be better off wedding your Papa, it has more chance of happiness. Take it from your old fool of a mother, as soon as the same laddy smells church bells chiming, he'll be flying out your door as fast as his Foxrock feet carry him. What have you to offer the likes of him and his, who, let me assure you, put more stock on a sizeable dowry than we can muster? Be under no illusions there, my lady.

I never suffer from any illusions, she informed me, bolder than brass and butter. You are the one who is under the illusion I could be your daughter, but I reject all your claims to my birth and status. I was reared by wolves in the black forests of Germany, it is where my lover and I must return, and there we shall die, each at the other's hand, a pact we make to sanctify our love and sacrifice for each other, which no one can desecrate by putting a stop to it.

Did you ever bear witness to such gobdaw mutterings? Amn't I right to have said no one could make head nor tail of what she was struggling to say, if there was struggle in it? I was determined to ask no questions nor heed a blind bit more of her wandering, when didn't she confront me, asking, was it you, Mama, gave Papa his disease?

That went beyond the beyond. That deserved a slap on the cunt. Don't think I'd hesitate. It was done to me, and I'd done it to her before, but on that occasion she, Beatrice, raised Cain to such an extent I thought her father was going to leave me – he wouldn't do that – and her brother went into such a paroxysm of crying you'd think it had been him that was hit. Nothing ever emerged after to elaborate on what I'd done, but I can say pretty much for certain that it was from the date of that slap, she never trusted me, nor I her. A child knows its mother, and she did me.

It was a pity things were as harsh as they were, for in some way I think I still expected her to at least have a fondness for me, even if not to love me. It's fair to say that was denied, and indeed so profoundly, I had to be on my permanent guard she might raise a hammer or hatchet and finish my head off as a smashed nest of bone and blood. In her ire I'd put nothing past her.

Why is she so angry? her father would ponder, what has set her in such a rage? Who can tell? I'd say, giving damn all away.

But he guessed. He always could. And I think it might have killed him. Might be killing him as we sit here, watching him die. She ruined our lives, my daughter. I cannot forgive her. We nearly did not make it across the Swiss border, him delaying till she was settled in a sanatorium he'd approve. I agreed we should be sure it was suitable. Christ, I'm not that black-hearted to leave her suffering from ill treatment or wandering round the French countryside in her shift and bare feet. I wouldn't do that to her. Would she, in her right mind, do it to me?

Yes, she would, probably, but still there's times I think of her and weep – not as sorely as her father, but I do genuinely weep for her. I'd look at her and wonder, who will want her in the end? What will become of her? I was thinking that, and maybe only that, on the day when we travelled to London to take the plunge at long last, our infants now well grown up, at a registry office in what's called Kens-ington. Himself mocked me, of course, saying I'd finally let the old sow Ireland devour me, I'd be a good married woman in the eyes of the law, if not in God's. I let him have his pleasure, for it was little enough to have the ring on my finger and the papers signed that might save myself, my son and above all my deranged daughter, growing more stricken by the day, from the workhouse.

There was money dribbling in from the books, and as I said to you, there had always been someone happy to stick their hand in their pocket and bail us out, but what if Himself were no more? What then? Eaten bread is soon forgotten, as our neighbour on Nun's Island, Mrs Madden, used say should be pinned to the chest of everyone tempted to do a good deed. She spoke the truth, I'm sure, but that's a rough lesson. Aren't they all – rough?

The rough with the smooth, they say, and the smoothest thing I'd ever felt was a man's pecker – again, a term from Mrs Madden, that she whispered once into my eager ear, and so I call it to myself from that day on.

He thought me the most wonderful of women when I kissed his, not that it hadn't been touched, roughly, smoothly, many times before, but this was the one he'd been waiting to hold him completely and never let go if it were humanly possible. It was love, I suppose, and at first sight you could call it, which sounds as good as it might get for any woman or man, but, like everything else, it comes at a cost, and mine was he'd never trust me to do as much as glimpse any other man, or he'd maintain I was trying to give him the blessing I'd bestowed that June day on himself. Did he have justification? Was it all one big act on his part to tie me down and do as he pleased?

If I gave him cause to suspect me, I'm of the conviction I only did so because that was his delight. And if it pleased him to picture me up to no good with other men, then I'd say with a mind like his, an imagination that could buy and sell me, you and the whole of Carraroe, it wasn't myself he dreamt rolling in their manly arms but himself, letting me do the dirty work he hadn't the cock for, much as he hungered for his own kind.

I never broke that bit of revelation to him before now, as he lies in his stupor, getting ready to face Satan, and between us and all harm, I hope it is Satan, for he will show him more sympathy than the Christ he has spent his adult years insulting. If I ever had doubts about the good Lord's existence, they're now becoming more certain, for a bolt of lightning has not hit me, streaming from the bed where himself is lying, meeting his end in Zurich. Could he foresee that end as he trooped the streets of Dublin as a boy, eyeing them, every alley, every brick, every broken window?

How could he? Should I ask him, hoping from somewhere in his soul I'll draw out an answer? Listen to him. Is that the river Liffey, or his blood flowing to a halt in his veins? The size of him, shrunken, yet I could trace every wailing woman he followed through every corpsehouse she ever haunted, bringing in her teeming cup the wine that will not quench the thirst of death and all its allies. He lies there, God forgive me, like a man debased, because he will not in his hour of agony call me by my name that I might, through his strength, summon powers that were powers that are powers that will forever be powers to save him from the fires where I fear he's going.

Priests – fuck them, you see they think they have us trapped at the end, but damn them instead, such virgins do not realise we who have known the body take flight in bed, one lust grown into the other, we are given what is denied to them – the sturdy wings of Archangels Michael and Gabriel to shelter us from their sermons and allow us to love and to sin and to be saved by sinning.

Who has told me this? He did, on the night we first touched. Little did that smart show-off understand that, when it came to getting your tongue around the right corners, I was so well ahead of him in that game. He needed to write it down, these screeds of our salvation, but me, sure all I had to do was breathe and it poured from me like water strong as drink. You see that's how I pulled off the miracle, miracle after miracle – I believed every word he told me, so I had the power to turn his lies, most beautiful lies, to truth.

And was he grateful? I think he was. Did he thank me? Do you know what – isn't he stretched here before me? So I'll ask him. Are you grateful? Do you thank me?

Not a sound. Not a sausage. Not a rasher nor an egg. Christ, the breakfasts the hard-working men of Galway could demolish. Boys fit for a day's work weaklings would take a fortnight to finish. They were carved from marble, and their hearts – they were the flowers of the forest, beating to their own music, ceasing when they chose to stop.

My most beloved, you are among their number. Let me feed you a last time, before you leave me. Do not leave me – I beg you, do not leave me. I will do whatever you ask to keep you by my side. I will free my son to be his own man. I will love my daughter, let her be what she is. Father, remember your children who need you. Husband, heed the wife who cries to you in this valley of tears, my life, my sweetness, my hope, most clement, most loving child of Adam and Eve.

What more does he want?

It goes without saying. Her, his daughter.

Let her loose. From far away in France, he will hear what she says. Fit her better it was the Rosary or her prayers she was reciting, but who am I to talk, I never let her learn them.

Again, all for him.

Let them be well suited. I could never come between them, try as I might. They can have each other now. And maybe she can do what I admit I cannot.

Save him.

CHAPTER THREE

Daughter
Beatrice

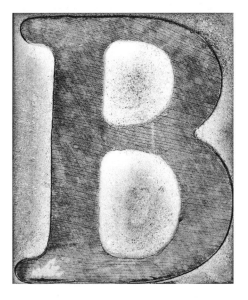

Ivar, France

My mother will visit me soon, I expect. She is a tennis champion, and this time of year, summer, she will be chasing one tournament after another, I expect. I have no interest in the game where she has made such a name for herself, so our conversation will, as it always has been – it will be limited, I expect. Yes, her diary is full, with commitments to travel and to play and to stay in expensive, well-run hotels, hundreds of servants attending to her every need, all very necessary for her continued well-being, I expect. My father indulges his wife, as only a rich husband could afford, I expect. Her dresses, both on and off the court, are beautifully made and fabulously expensive, costing more than a year of a doctor's salary, certainly doctors who are unlucky enough to find themselves working in this establishment, I expect. Anyway, Mama is a woman who enjoys being spoilt, and father enjoys spoiling her, so she would be, as he would be, furious to hear me even hint of her extravagance, I expect. She has simply never learned the value of money, and she never will now, I expect.

There is something odd about all I'm telling you, in strictest confidence of course. Have you noticed? I'm certain you have, I'm sure you are sharp as a knife. You are remarking on how sure I am this is summertime, and if it is so, why am I stuck in a room? It is a room, isn't it? And I live in a hotel, don't I?

A hotel that is not quite so grand compared to where my mother lodges on her travels through Europe, but I am, as always, content with my lot and do not envy her a life of wandering from one capital to another, eating, sleeping, causing riot and havoc, blasting tennis balls to kingdom come if that should help her triumph in the games she plays, rounding up innocent and guilty to come and watch as she decrees they should, applauding, cheering when they're told, the mob obeying as she demands they do. As far away as I am in rural France, I can see here the havoc she creates when she decides to visit and destroy wherever her heart's desire leads her. A noisy woman, a strange woman indeed, but not a dancer. Dear me, no.

That was the first thing my teacher observed about her and told me immediately. Mama overheard and was furious. She went into quite a frenzy, as could be her wont. I had seen her in a temper before – hadn't we all? But this was of an exceptional violence.

My instructor, a frail lady, who now walked only by aid of a cane, was clearly in fear of her life and really had to defend herself as best she could with that cane against my mother's pushing and kicking, while screaming blue murder in a language I did not know, nor could I make any effort to have her calm down until an idea struck me. I might turn on Mama with all the ferocity she herself was summoning from whatever source inside her and I should direct these exertions towards her so that, physically, she could concentrate her attack on someone other than the old ballerina.

It worked, but here's the weird thing. As she lashed out against me, people came running to her defence, holding me back, and when they succeeded in doing so, from their behaviour towards me, I was regarded as the sole villain of the piece, mauling my mother, her brutal assault on a woman who was herself a fragile remnant from an earlier age, that was quite forgotten, and when I looked to this delicate soul for confirmation of what had happened and that I was only doing my best to protect her, hadn't she vanished into thinnest air, leaving me without a witness to testify why I'd had to stoop to these impetuous blows and put an end to Mama's antics?

She was clever enough to deny all to my father and brother, so they were suspicious of me, suggesting that maybe I should stop going to these classes as they might be exhausting and making me conduct myself in such outlandish fashion as they now accused me of behaving.

What would you have me do then for exercise? I challenged her, play tennis like you? Like me? What are you talking about? she dared ask.

You well know what. I let her understand she was not to take me for a fool, the whole world is aware that tennis is how you've chosen to waste your life – neglecting us, your children, discarding the needs of my father, all to satisfy your vanity and be acclaimed for your athletic brilliance on the courts.

The tennis courts? I heard her repeating, where I have never set foot in my entire life. I can no longer deal with this, I cannot take this insanity a moment longer, if your father will not confront it and do what must be done, Archie, will you take charge and save your sister's life, and spare what's left of your mother's sanity? I swear it is running out, second by second, as we speak. Did you hear what she says about me – a tennis champion? Where under Jesus does she get these notions from? There's only one source, and he's there sitting on a chair, listening to all this, and I swear he's smiling. What's there to smile at? What's the fun in this? How can you laugh at your mad daughter?

I would not give Mama the satisfaction of proving her right by lifting the nearest object and hurling it hard in her direction, although you would agree her outburst sorely tempted me to do so. But like my father, I am a creature of graceful restraint, and so I merely smiled and nodded in his direction. She does this to infuriate me, my mother said, they both do, sending secret signals, one to the other, but I will not give in to the temptation they put before me. I will ignore them, as they deserve.

I'm smiling because it amuses me how our daughter sometimes can access my dreams, Father explained, and this tennis – anchoring you to a tennis court, seeing you there, well, it's as if we have stumbled on the same connection, for you, my dear, have often come to me in my sleep as the great French player, Suzanne Lenglen, La Divine. You are where our daughter's agility, her speed, her flamboyance come from, and no mistake.

La Divine? That is who you think I am? No, I don't think so, she said, not that, not in dreams, but in reality a laugh, a mockery, a dirty great Galway sow, fit only to be prodded and poked by you pair that see me as being there for your ridicule and a good time had by all who came to the party to jeer. Are you proud of yourselves? Proud? he repeated. Are you happy that all your brains let you do is sneer at me, a woman who's done neither of you any wrong? Suzanne Lenglen, is that what you make of me? she asked, but they did not reply.

A woman too busy showing her legs, Mama continued, and her arse to the nations of the world to be considered as anything other than a word I won't stain my soul using, since in this family there are too many souls – well, there's certainly one – stinking to high heaven, looking for punishment to be rained down on his head and the heads of any tragic enough to call him their own. Laugh on, laugh on, it will soon be on the other side of your face.

She was very upset, my mother. There would be no denying that.

Perhaps that is why she has not yet paid me a visit. But

she will come soon. I am certain she has not forgotten me. She prides herself that we both have ferocious memories. And my brother, he can recall, he claims, the day he was born. That, you know, is an affliction to bear as much as forgetfulness.

I was married once, or nearly so, to an Irishman, a Dubliner, and he too was stricken with the plague of seeing everything, hearing everything, tasting – touching – smelling everything. What became of him? I wonder. Does he ask ever, What became of her? Her, me – what is the difference? This, he told me, was the kind of question he most liked to pose, but I could tell what he really desired, and that was to see me piss.

I declined to satisfy this proclivity, but not without much persuasion from this gentleman that this was a habit customary in his neck of the woods. You mean, I asked, in Dublin men are inclined to spy on ladies relieving themselves in what they imagine to be the privacy of their bathroom, but which are in fact more open to the world than the most squalid pissoirs? No, not through the whole of Dublin, but in certain suburbs it is the fashion, he assured me, most especially his own, Foxrock, a highly desirable quarter that houses some of the best families associated with the Church of Ireland or the Royal Bank, architects and dentists also being most welcome within this salubrious vicinity.

Someday I must take you there, he suggested, but I declined firmly, and none too politely.

Do I strike you as the kind of woman who might indulge another's perversions? I asked. He defended himself from any such charge of indecency, claiming a fascination with the urinary tracts of females was a winning aspect of any normal man who liked his fair share of female flesh sourly scented with her own waste material.

Call me old-fashioned and a tad too attuned to the riddles of the Irish, but I could see clearly enough where this paradox was leading, and I was determined to halt the conversation between us. I do not care for normal men then, if that is how they court the opposite sex, I retorted, give me a pervert – or a pervert in your eyes anyway – on all romantic occasions. I shall bear that in mind, he informed me. Do, I encouraged him, and perhaps you might let the people of Foxrock reconsider what they judge to be decent behaviour as it is conducted between members of the opposite sex. There is no opposite sex in Foxrock, he let me know, there are only windows. Widows? I asked him, only widows? Has there been a war, or some epidemic, that only carried off the male of the species? I said. Windows, not widows, he instructed me, I made no mention of widows, though we have our fair share of them, and not one has ever been burned alive, to the best of my knowledge, but I could stand corrected, he admitted.

Burned? The widows? I asked, who would encourage such barbarity? The Hindus have a form of ceremony that corresponds, he instructed me, I believe they call it suttee, but I hesitate to describe our ways in similar terms. Why? I wanted to know. I mistakenly thought, he admitted, it was Foxrock's way of saluting its tribute to the British presence in India. So many of our residents held sway on that part of the Asian subcontinent. My childhood memories are replete with umbrellas of all shades standing desolately in a hollowed-out elephant's foot. I used imagine the brollies come to life and charge through the princely residences of our village, goring my enemies to death with their powerful tusks, staining their ivory red. But this was simply not the case. There were other, less obvious reasons to fear fire in Foxrock.

He enlightened me why. Something remarkably similar to suttee had happened a few years before he was born, so although he had no direct recollection of the event, it had caused sufficient scandal to be talked about, the pros and cons weighed, the right and wrong of the matter settled, or questioned, for years.

He was reluctant to call the event by its Hindu name, for this self-consummation involved a woman, a Catholic, yes, but not a widow. No, this individual had prepared and set herself alight on her own funeral pyre. Her reasons for committing this apparently unhinged act were made quite clear in a letter she left behind to account for this more than a little bizarre exploit. She hated her husband, and this was her rather extreme way of being rid of him. He'd long been a disgrace to his own family, his father a quantity surveyor, and his mother, of saintly disposition, a nurse. Their son had travelled throughout Ireland, using the alias of the Sheik of Araby, to save bringing disrepute on the more rational members of his kith and kin. His act involved conjuring magic tricks. All the time he accompanied himself with mouth music that he claimed to have been taught to him in Arabia by a master of the Eastern Arts, calligraphy and falconry being his particular areas of expertise.

No one ever saw the Sheik tame as much as a robin, so the latter practice had to be taken as assumed. His handwriting scrawled in so many directions a career as a schoolmaster was out of the question, but it may be such a style perfectly accommodated the beauties of the Arabic alphabet, maybe ever stretching to a proficiency in Egyptian hieroglyphics. Who can tell? Suffice to say a neighbour well-versed in the intricacies of Ireland's hidden cultures identified the sounds emitted from the Sheik's mouth while in a trance, performing his bag of tricks. They were ascertained to be nothing but a form of singing once common enough in the parts of the island where Gaelic is spoken and identified as sean-nós, meaning old style, providing much noise and little pleasure.

Confronted with proof of his deception that he hailed from royal, oriental blood, that in short he had faked his name, his career and his art, the so-called Sheik of Araby declared it an outrage to have been so uncovered and humiliated, he would thus abandon Dublin and go to live in a cave near Athlone. His poor wife had endured

much through her nomadic life with this reckless vaga-
bond, but the threat of Athlone, and she knew whereof
she spoke, provoked her into choosing a hideous death
by self-immolation, welcoming the hungry flames licking
her to hell, since suicide was a mortal sin.

Yet was it suicide? The very fact she chose and conducted such an elaborate method of exterminating herself,
well, did that not betoken a mind that made its decision
in a detailed, perfectly logical fashion? Others argued pas-
sionately that the very violence of her exit was sign she
had surely taken utter leave of her senses, and the poor dear
must not be condemned for her own reckless execution.
For God's sake, pity her.

That was the response, by and large, among the Protestant side of the tribe in Foxrock, but of course in Ireland, no
matter where you point the finger, you'll find the opposite
view in some form or other to some degree, small or large,
and in this case, as in so many, things were complicated by
the fact the woman herself was Catholic. The long and the
short of this all came down then to one deeply contested
fact – not was she in her right mind when she set a match
to the paraffin, but by writing that letter in her own hand,

abandoning her spouse, was it divorce and not suicide she was seeking?

Well, her people knew where they stood on that issue. And the consensus was total. The slut insulted the truth of her faith. No room for doubt. She was not to be forgiven. Not our way. And the populace agreed her ashes be denied burial in the waters of the River Liffey or any of its tributaries, or indeed the wide expanse of the Irish Sea itself. Let that be a lesson to all sinners who would defy the sacred oath of the marriage vows. The Sheik of Araby – he continued with the old, assumed name, out of grief – he was complaining he found himself at a serious loss as to what then to do with her remains. For pure convenience he'd kept the ashes in that elephant's foot mentioned earlier, together with a circumference of umbrellas.

What became of her dust, he couldn't say for sure, but it was rumoured that when they built a Roman Catholic Church in Foxrock, her spirit haunted it, laughing uproariously at inappropriate moments of the Mass, particularly in funeral services.

The stories of my lover's youth were, more or less, all like this, obsessed with death and ghosts, and here's another strange detail about them, if bloody parasols or brollies in general did not feature, then you can be quite assured ladders will. We had arranged to go out walking one afternoon, and then drink tea in a sweet little establishment my father had been asked to leave for insulting the honour of France by farting deliberately at the mere mention of Joan of Arc, claiming he heard voices in the explosion, whose they were he was not allowed to reveal at the behest of the Saviour. Out – out, the owners demanded. But he finished his tea, stole a saucer and did not pay the bill. Such nerve, that wonderful man. Will he come and visit me? This word he is dying, it's lies. How can he be put in the earth, when he is the earth? Is that not what he has told me, in our secret way, and I have believed it to be gospel truth? Father, wake up, sing – sing 'The Sheik of Araby'.

I'm the Sheik of Araby,
Your love belongs to me.
At night when you're asleep,
Into your tent I'll creep.

The stars that shine above
Will light our way to love.
You rule the world with me,
I'm the Sheik of Araby.

When you're asleep – sleep, sleep. Into your tent, I'll creep – creep, creep. Wake up, father. I have to tell you this story, about your acolyte, about his habit of walking the streets of Paris hauling a ladder after him and why he does so. His answer surprised me. While some do like to bring their children or dogs, even their cats and lobsters, out for a stroll, he brought a ladder for the exercise of carrying it, and for the company of its conversation. Are you telling me two things? I inquired. First is it always the same ladder we are talking about? And if it is, secondly, do you regard this object as some sort of companion?

He confirmed, yes, it was indeed identical, always the same one, but declined to be so definite as to why it was frequently in his presence. Companion – well, it sounded not quite right. Too intimate? Perhaps. And yet he had come to depend on this ladder as a comfort much as one would a beloved pet that stands close by in times of need.

Do you have a particular reason for bringing it with us on the day that's in it? I demanded to know. Yes, I do, he softly whispered, as a romantic gesture, I would like us to climb the Eiffel Tower.

There are times that individual knows exactly the way to my heart. Had I somehow, somewhere, let slip that this artifice, this miracle of French engineering, this most elegant masterpiece, I have long adored it as an object of brilliant genius? Ask me what it is I most covet in the great city of Paris. It is not the prized tapestries of the Virgin and the Unicorn in the Musée de Cluny, although as a child I did see a unicorn in a field – where was it? Normandy, a little village called Boisny – but on investigation it proved to be nothing more than a pedlar's goat, milked near to extinction to sate his permanent thirst and offered to us to buy for the price of a bottle of wine and a plate of venison stew? We declined the offer, my parents did, despite the protestation of Archie and myself. He put me in here, in this hotel, my brother. Why? Perhaps in revenge that I informed him his precious unicorn was nothing more than a shitty farmyard beast.

No, not the Cluny and all its treasures, these I would

decline, as I would the grave of Napoleon, and all the silks and laces of the ladies wandering serenely through the Sundays of the racecourse at Longchamp, nervous as newborn fillies, highly strung like my good self, in most urgent need of minding. I would reject the delicate motorcars that could be most severely crushed by collision with their own like or swerving suddenly to miss a pack of cackling geese sauntering down a country road in the Auvergne, never feeling such speed or causing such mayhem, bloodied as the bodies, headless in the Vendée, priests, nuns, bishops, chopped to little pieces fed to fatten the pigs, the goats, the unicorns of the district.

Then what about Chardin, painter of the ordinary, rendering it sublime? Look at the boy building a tower of playing cards; one feel, one breath, it falls apart, as he and all his works will when age touches him? None of these has my heart, my soul. I declare allegiance only to the Eiffel Tower.

Why? Because I firmly maintain that in another life I built it. This feat is all the more remarkable when you consider that now, as in my past, I suffered most painfully from fear of heights. A robust dashing young peasant fellow as I was then, I had made my way – from Boisny again – to stake my claim and gain a fortune in Paris. My mother's tears blessed me as I left our hovel, and she cried out in warning after me, remember you can barely stand on a chair without fainting, you take after my side of the family, do not forget you are terrified–

I blocked out what she specified my terror was, for if truth be told, everything was foreign and frightening to me in this great city, where I found employment in the construction of Monsieur Eiffel's great work. It must have been the life for me, certainly it removed all traces of vertigo, for I lasted in the job and I have not the slightest recollections of panic as I ascended into the sky, erecting this most beautiful of structures, sure of my footing to the extent that I could watch workers tumble to their death and not blink an eyelid nor feel the slightest tremor of alarm, but instead blessed them and wished their souls to heaven.

So much of my life in that time, it is dark as night to me and I do not like to probe its mysteries too deeply, since I have trouble enough with my own sanity as things now stand, but I know why I experience such affection for the tower and the man who entrusted me when I was a young boy to construct it, taking from me the paralysing sense I would never climb as high as I might have dreamt I could.

Then I died and turned into a girl, my career as a labourer was over. I told no one about my secret life, although I think my father guessed what kind of workman I had been. Why else would he tell me filthy songs and stories strong enough to churn my stomach? Why else would he give me his taste for kidneys or tripe and onions? Why else would he confess in drink, for my ears only to hear, the way his father forced his mother to do her duty, when she could barely talk after childbirth, let alone walk? Why else would he tell me his father loved to suckle his wife's breasts, stroking her arse, calling her Mammy? Why else would he teach me the sacred oaths, to keep always under my breath, that a man could call a woman but never in her hearing, unless he wished permanent banishment from her bed? Why else but that he, and he alone, saw the shadow of the cock between my legs and cared for me as the son my brother failed to be?

Why did I start calling those terrible names at Mama and keep on repeating them, turning every inch of her pale with shock, as she well realised who it was could alone teach me them to punish her as he did when they fucked? Did the young man carrying the ladder hoping we'd climb the Eiffel Tower, did he have – could he have any notion of this? I'd say not, but who knows?

All and sundry were staring at us, him, me and the ladder sauntering through Paris, the three of us. I might have forgotten what our purpose was, had he not asked me in his usual manner of wanting to know more on the subject of my father, what was Papa's opinion, did I know, of the Tower – marvel or monstrosity? This could not be allowed to pass without a bit of sport to entertain myself. I told him that while I had no knowledge about my father in this respect, my mother had expressed her opinion in no uncertain terms. It would be fair to say this did not spark a rush of interest. Still, I let him in on the fact that she found it a bit of an eyesore, and not a patch on what she'd seen as a girl in Connaught, or more specifically Connemara. He did not have the good grace to wonder what that might be, so I had to enlighten him it was not an architectural nor mathematical extravagance, but a monument, another kind of monument to the millions who lost their lives starving in the Irish Famine. And it consisted only of skulls, heaps and heaps and heaps of skulls reaching up into the sky, polished white by the rain and sleet and snow of

Galway winters than which there never were damper nor hasher, as if these dead took their revenge through inflicting this most savage climate.

He believed me. Papa, he did. Would that not leave you laughing your arse out? Would that not have you splitting your sides and spitting tobacco? Would that not drive you to drink and put a giddy-on to your gallop? At the news of this, would you not notice the earth spinning and the moon colliding? Would you credit that was the end of the world, for I never set eyes on him or the ladder or the Eiffel Tower again? I must have somehow shamed him and his breed, his lock, stock and barrel, his bones, his bible, the faith of his fathers, that did next to nothing to remedy the suffering Irish a century ago, and he knew it. Hadn't I behaved like my mother's daughter, and he left me for it. And when I informed her of this, did she thank me for my loyalty? Did she pity me for my loss? When I told her I had proved myself odd as Aunt Gertie with her arse out the window so no man would marry me and I'd be marooned alone, did she comfort me with sweet assurances I was a beautiful girl that fellows would die for and that children would flow from me?

If she did, I could not hear her. Instead I saw the look she exchanged with my brother, and to my grief, I knew she hates me, aye, this woman hates me, and for why? Because I was born.

Forgive me, Mama – do. Come and visit me. Why does she not? Was it because I called her names? I will not do that again. I promise. I keep my promise, as I was taught to do. I put away my toys. I chew my food. I am an exceptionally obedient child. A very, very well behaved girl. And my fiancé, he used tell me, he used to be my fiancé, I am beautiful. All dancers are. All dancers are cracked. A bit cracked. Like an egg.

I remember eggs. For years, she would make me eat one. Boiling it in scalding water. Cracking open its gentle shell, then leaving it to stand, white and naked. The sharpest knife in our house cuts it in pieces and she shovels it – she always says that – shovels it – into my cup where butter waits to be melted into the beautiful smell. Then she fetches my favourite spoon – the littlest one with a man crossed-armed at its top, an apostle she calls him – and feeds me, making sure I swallow every mouthful. And as I break my fast, she tells me the names of Galway, the Claddagh and Taylor's Hill, Nun's

Island and Eyre Square, towns with lovely sounds like Spiddal and Oughterard, Moycullen and Rahoon, which is when she always stops, repeating Rahoon, Rahoon, Rahoon, and some days she cries.

When I was old enough to notice her tears, I asked her why, one day. Because at this minute, she told me straight, I would like to go home, because I am tired in my bones, tired of your father and all he's made me do, though Christ knows I was willing to be out of and far away from that nest of vipers, Ireland, but he sometimes forgets how much I sacrificed to do his bidding. I left behind my family, my faith, my home town, my heart that is breaking to see again where I belong, the girls all dark and Spanish, the black-haired fellows, beautiful, to take your breath away and put it back again, their tongues in your mouth, tasting your tonsils, the shower of them, good for only one thing, thanks be to Christ and his crucified mother – didn't she suffer what he suffered? For they are the best at it above all men from other nations or cities of the earth. Well, so they like to tell you, and my arse is parsley. Eat up your eggs, it's Easter Day, finish it for luck. I've sourced some lamb, and for your father I will roast it to perfection.

She did so, but always ran herself down as a cook. Whatever else he sees in me, she would ever tell strangers, it's not because I am a dab hand with the grub. No, she fed us as best she could, and I would not fault her food, were she not in the business of trying to poison me. My father tried to talk me out of what he called – what was it? Bad thoughts? No, nor mad either, but what he described as dreams, mad dreams, nightmares that came from nowhere and I must not believe in them, for they would take me from them, carry me away, and I might not come back from where they led me.

She would simply not tolerate such nonsense, as she called it, from me no more than she would allow anything be wasted that could be put in your mouth and swallowed. But I will grow fat, I protested. What – fat as me? she snarled. I would not give her the satisfaction of rising to her bait. Instead I declared that I was in on her plan to kill me. How will I do that? she demanded. You will eat me alive, I told her, you will dine on my flesh, and you will serve it to my father and my brother. It will turn my father into a woman, for you will only serve him my breast and a slice of my anus. He will relish the smell of it and devour it, not noticing, in his delight, his knob is no more. You will stuff into Archie's mouth my elbow, my eyes – and here's what's best of all, that's when he will at long last start seeing you for what you are, Mama, a cannibal from Connemara, where Father says they eat their young out of starvation and where you say you picked up the habit of disembowelling.

I don't observe you too deficient in bodily parts, she retorted, and that is when I took that knife – the sharpest in the house – and heard her scream I was going to stab her.

Not a bit of it. I simply asked my father and my brother if they would like to shave me between my legs and make cufflinks or a tiepin out of my silver down? Was it silver or gold? Was it a strange alloy of both? Do you know I can't tell you, for it has been years now since I probed in that secret place where unborn babies lie unhatched waiting for the greatest of the gods to visit and ravish me in the shape of some bull or bird or other, depending on his mood.

Had I a choice, which would I prefer? A bull, when I feel my mother hold sway within me, and my blood has all the hunger of the men of Connaught, longing to be satisfied up their arses by eleven inches of ivory stolen from a temple on the Nile dedicated to the goddess Isis so as to satisfy the lust of Queen Victoria, the harlot. A bird, when I feel my father caress me with his wing, feathered, his down the soft roughness of Donegal tweed, and I would let him ravish me if only to be assured he can take the form of a god, for they must not be judged by the rules of human contact.

He must not be judged, my father. He must be eternally extolled, my father. Who is it I see bestride the colossus of my cunt but my father? Where dragons lurch breathing my mother's fire, who is my protector but my father? Where thieves lie in wait to ambush and divest me of my armour, who is my champion, only my father? If the skies were to open and great Zeus himself threaten to burn me to a cinder, who will be my shield? Yes, my father. When my brother drinks himself into sour stupor, who burns with righteous anger at his son's strangeness? My father, my father. Who reads to me arcane secrets buried in the earth's frozen wastes? My father. Who will take my hand and lead me from this exile back to where my chosen people long for me, surely? It must be my father. You cannot lie there, spent, dead to the world, waiting only for death, in that lonely bed, for that is what I do, father. Get up, get up and see your daughter, my father. See yourself in her and save the two of us. Here I'll place a knife – the sharpest in our house – place it in your hand. What will you do with it?

It is Easter Day, and he carved the lamb. Our neighbours eat goose, fatty, smelly goose, laying eggs on their table, eggs for luck, if you were to believe their lies, and we never do. Though it is sweetly herbed and cooked as we all like it, the lamb sheds its blood beneath my father's knife. Red trickles on our plates, and we would lick them clean, loving blood, still we are not savage but civilised beings who know what to do at table, and so we use white bread to lap the liquid, consecrated offering, who could it be possibly grows annoyed at this? Perhaps it is myself. I eat a morsel and wash it down with a mouthful of wine. Good wine. My father's choice, an excellent vintage. He toasts my mother, my brother, myself. I down another bite. I swallow the staff of life. My mother compliments me on my appetite.

I let this pass without looking at her, without speaking back, without touching her foul skin, tasting her fetid breath, for I have, as they say, other fish to fry since I now know what is happening inside my belly. The lamb is growing back into its living shape. I can feel it sniff my internal organs – heart and spleen, kidneys and lungs – rejecting, mercifully, to dine on my body, but I know it needs water, so I quench its thirst with water, loads of water, a basin full, a lough full if necessary.

Was there too much salt on the beast? She'll drink the city dry, my mother notices. At last I smile, and she is relieved I am not, as she now says so often, having one on my turns. I let her lose her panic and then I say, May I ask if we have in the kitchen any grass? I would like to eat some grass. Why? my brother asks. Why not? my mother answers, how long has she been waiting to spring that surprise? Isn't it only right and fitting that she should look for hay – no, maybe she should be more demanding and insist on the flowers of the fields, because there we can oblige her.

She plucks lilies from their vase. A cup of primroses is poured in front of me. I am only sorry, she laments, that our bill of fare cannot stretch to more exotic blooms, but there it is, the time of year defeats us, so I trust she will forgive us, little Miss Bo Peep here, and the herd of sheep who, if I may hazard a guess and I think I will be correct since I am getting wise to her little ways, the flock that now feeds inside her – am I right? Of course I am. They are hungry, they want grass, the green grass of Erin, you could sing that if you put a tune to it, and Jesus, am I sick to the tonsils of listening to your refrains. Will they never cease? Will you ever give it a rest? If you confound me for the delight of doing so, has it not now dawned on you I am up to each and every one of your devices and I fall for none of them? Has that not at last hit you?

The chair I was sitting on was sturdy. I could feel it bear my weight, and it was as if its wood became part of what most turned my stomach against myself and this woman who bore me. Its legs, its arms – silent, static. I was waiting for them to do something, do anything. They did not disappoint me, for the next thing was they had jerked me – hurled me perhaps more correctly – to my feet with such force I nearly felt my head beating against the wall opposite, and I let out an almighty roar that could wake the dead if I or they were so inclined to believe in resurrections, the day that was, as I said, in it.

On my feet I stopped swaying before my brother reached me, and that damned unmannerly chair, that wonderful chair, what did it do next but leap from the floor straight into my arms. Whatever force propelled it must have been powered by fire, for I could sense it scorching me, burning a hole through me, and it was absolutely necessary that I by some superhuman effort – it now weighed more than my brother – toss it away from me in whatever direction it decided to fly. Was it really any surprise it should find my mother's face? Should any have been shocked that the chair screamed, You have long had this coming? For your arse, sitting on top of me, smelling as it does of rancid lard, for all your cruelty, for your neglect, for your hatred, fuck you. Do you not deserve this magic when the furniture, the very chairs in your house, would throttle you, if they had a chance? Now, given it, they will teach you a lesson you will never forget, Mama, never, never ever.

No, I won't, that's all she said, nor will you, she added, and my brother took me away from the table, in case it too sided with me against this terrible woman.

Commit her, I heard her tell my father, have her committed, or commit me, she asked.

And still he said nothing.

For a man so versed in the wisdom of all words, a mind so fashioned according to all the most elaborate and illuminating schemes of things – he was more than the author, he was the book itself that passes understanding, and only he and I knew such things – my father was my father was my father, I expect. In this instance he could be no more than my father. So what was done had to be done, and, as they say in Ballyhaunis, remove her immediately from the field of play. I have never been to Ballyhaunis, but I was removed. Bag, baggage and ladder to this spot where you find me, and my fiancé did not come to save me.

If he did, I wonder would he notice the old woman who sometimes sits in the same room as I do? Would he find out who she might be? It is not my mother – I'd recognise her. Far gone I may be, but not that far gone. She smokes incessantly, and her voice is harsh. I sometimes have great difficulty deciphering what she says. Are you Irish? That was one of her first questions. I am when I'm not, and I'm not when I am, I answered, hoping this riddle would put a stop to that one's gallop. I cannot fathom you at all there, she said, but I think I know what you're up to, talking in such fashion. Is this a way of making strange with me?

That's an expression baffles me, I told her, I have not the slightest notion what you mean. Indeed and you do, she declared, wasn't it often said about you when you were a child, frightened of strangers, crying to be taken from them, happy only in your parents' arms? Am I right? Is that not what is meant by making strange? If it is, I told her, it's still new to me, but how would you know what way I conducted myself as an infant?

That would be telling, she confused me, and isn't it best not to say a word when you don't know who's listening, and what it is they want to hear? She clammed up then and lit her cigarette from the one that was burning between her fingers, stamping it out with her black, flat shoe on the ground. You'll have to forgive me sitting here keeping you company, puffing the hours away, she admitted, as you've noticed I couldn't be without tobacco. It's the life of me. An awful habit I know, but don't we all succumb to it, smoking like chimneys, women like ourselves, light on our feet, up on our toes, dancers, a breed apart?

Is that what you are? I wanted to know. It's what I used to be, she replied, until the weight, the aches, the pains, the hump on my back, the rheum in my eyes – they all conspired to still me. Now, if I could put one foot in front of the other, I'd try to convince myself I was stepping out onstage with the Russian imperial ballet, ready to execute the most fastidious of steps, all for the glory of the men who loved me. Tell me, have you ever been so loved?

I felt such interrogation the height of impertinence and strongly considered passing on giving even the most cursory reply, but there was something about this old doll and the way she used her compact mirror to powder her face, holding it at such an angle that my own reflection slipped into the side of her glass, I felt for some reason honour bound to let her know that yes, I had been loved.

I suppose you know, I informed her, that beyond these walls there's a war raging, spreading havoc through all the nations of Europe, blighting this generation and all others that will succeed it? I have a passing knowledge of such matters, she replied, cool as a cucumber stripped of its skin and its seeds, dressed in the proper manner, reeking of cider vinegar – the only way my father would deign to digest such a vegetable. A passing knowledge? I mocked her gently, I compliment your powers of selective hearing, my good lady, since the rest of the continent is rife with rumours of horrors being committed that none can comprehend – why have armies sunk to such brutalities against their fellow humans?

I know well what's being done out there, she let me

know, how could I not when olive trees are shedding blood from their leaves, the birds of the air abandon their songs, and the silence, that silence, drives me into these four high walls, that I might block my ears to the infinite weeping of those born to die too young, too young, too young like yourself.

That's where you're wrong, I corrected her, I am not dying. I only have your word for this, she replied, I would need more concrete proof. Then are you prepared to hear and believe my deepest secret? I threatened. No, she said, for I have been well warned against you and your powers of lying. Did you not make a mockery of a poor Dublin lad from the wilds of the village of Foxrock, demanding in return for your hand he fetch you all the bricks used to construct the Eiffel Tower? No bricks were used, I defended myself. Didn't he learn that the hard way, as all do who are touched by us? she hinted. But I missed the clue and heard only what she continued to reveal as she informed me this was how you lost him, this mockery, this was why he tossed to one side any desire to wed you, but in place of that, he pursued your father in hope of marrying him. He was rejected by that good man in deference to you, his daughter. Are you proud of yourself?

That is none of your business, but I must insist, I told her, insist you tell me how you know so much about me and my past. Your present and your future too, she added, if truth be told.

So you can tell me what will befall, you are a seer, a prophetess, is that what you're now claiming? I asked her, and she nodded her head, saying nothing. How do you know me? I repeated. Because I am your vassal, your serf, your slave, you have won me in the war, isn't that why it's being fought? She challenged me, most fiercely. And it was then I convinced myself she had me rumbled.

How are you certain that the world is in convulsions because of me? I demanded she tell. They speak of nothing else in Poland, she whispers. I have never been there, I let her know. In Russia, in Estonia, mothers pray to your icon, she admits. I have never been painted, I let her know that as well. Your face adorns a million walls in Germany, she tells me. And it is most cruelly mocked by the addition of a moustache, is it not? I question her. England's king abandons the realm for the sake of a woman, she confides. Is she me? I want to know. Yes, she sighs. When has this all happened? I demand an answer. While you were sleeping, locked in this castle, she tells me, waiting for your father. To come and rescue me? I inquire. No, waiting for him to die, and he will die, she assures me.

This is when I hear a scream that shakes me to the core, but herself sitting opposite, this hideous old fool, it does not take a wrinkle out of her, although she is more lined, more ancient than the Rock of Gibraltar, and all she says is my name, Beatrice, Beatrice, is that right? Am I guessing correctly? Do you know why I may have stumbled on this? But I refused to answer. I will not fall for that familiar ruse as a way of humiliating me.

Once, in school, every girl in my classroom claimed that she was called Beatrice, either at birth or as a term of endearment. It was too ridiculous for words, this apparent coincidence, and I refused to believe them, so they called out to our teacher, letting her know I was calling them liars, demanding was I the only one among them with the right to bear the name? She is showing off again, they chorus, she is trying to be different. And so I must be punished. How?

Is it to be tied to this place for eternity listening to the endless prattle of an old fool as she sits choking herself to death – it could not come quickly enough – urging me to take on board the minutiae of her existence, as if such details conformed to a marked measure with those that go to make up my own story? Or is that another matter entirely?

I should ask the nurse when she fetches my dinner, but I'm not sure if I speak her dialect of French, or indeed if she is not herself deaf and dumb, for she never does anything nor says one civilised word of conversation, but grunts instead as if I were an animal. Perhaps I am an animal – she knows something I do not. What kind? Might she let me in on the secret of what she sees or indeed smells in me? A camel or kangaroo? A bear or a gazelle?

No, never a gazelle, I have grown too lame to be that, and my dancing days are over. But I clearly have about me the stench of the farmyard. That is why they feed me such volumes of pig. Every meal of fat is forced down my gullet. There are nights in dreams I imagine I am growing a snout. Complain, you would say – insist on fruit and vegetables. Plead for even a little wing of chicken. But such things are beyond me now, for I feel my days are numbered. Ask the ancient fool sitting opposite me to earn her keep and let her do the necessary – finish me off, but she won't. I notice she can guzzle as good as the rest of them, but there I run into difficulty, for it appears no one can actually see this bygone relic but myself, and there is great reluctance to admit she dwells amongst us. Once upon a time we could have smuggled her into our daily existence, in the days before rationing and shortage, but not now when it is necessary to be somebody in case they come looking for whatever tribe takes their fancy for disposal, depending on your luck, good and bad.

I explained this complicated situation to her – or at least I made some attempt but she halted me, waving me into silence. It is not at all complicated, she smiled, the brute fact is I come and go as I please. We are under lock and key here, I retaliated. Not me, I'm not, she was now positively beaming, you may be, but I am under special dispensation, so I am permitted to open doors without a key, walk through walls as if they were carved from mere gossamer, and should I feel confined, then the roof itself will let me ascend through its beams and slates, if straw is no longer the fashion. There is, my dear, she tells me, an obvious reason why they cannot see me – frequently I am not there. The consequence is you are regarded as what, I believe, in legal terms, is all too often dismissed as an unreliable witness. Irritating, it must be, the only consolation is that I believe you – I know you always tell things as you see they are. In short you are a girl who tells the truth, and that is why I visit you.

Will you tell my mother? I plead with her, will you tell her to come and see me? Bring my brother. Bring my father.

She cannot do that. He is much too ill. In the hospital, in Zurich. Miles away. That is where they all are. It is safe there. In the mountains. In the lakes. In the rivers. In the snow. Is it snowing in his room, my father's? Does the snow come through the window, falling on his bed, and does he think it is white as a cat, or a rabbit, coming to take his soul? I would like to be my daddy's girl and hear him singing lullabies. Or he could tell me silly stories about the neighbours who surrounded them in his dear old dirty Dublin.

Tell me, Papa, about Kitty Maguire. Kitty Maguire sat on the fire, the fire was too hot, she sat on the pot, the pot was too round, she sat on the ground, the ground was too flat, she sat on the cat, and the cat ran away – the cat ran away – the cat ran – where did the cat run? Do you not know?

Does he not know? Why aren't you speaking? Why is she crying, my mother? Why are you crying, Archie?

In this house we have built from the weapons of our words, why is there silence? Will this mean that our walls fall asunder? Will our windows crack and our doors fall open – close the door, darken the windows, that's what's done in Galway, isn't it, Mama? That's how we free his spirit – or do they do the opposite? Unbolt everything, draw back the snib. Let it fly from us, his soul. No, cast nets and catch it, hold him to our breast, get up from the grave, Papa, throw off the soil of earth, rise, man, and give us a bit of your blather, dazzle us with the dirt you've gathered on high and low, let your soul magnify, fill the hungry with plenty, protect Israel, your servant – is it over, is he breathing?

She's back, the old witch. Yes, he's breathing, she tells me. Where were you? I ask her. Near enough, she teases. Are you sure? I quiz her. Positive, she informs me. How can you be so? I wonder. I took a mirror, would you credit this? she wonders. I held it before his mouth. And did you see his breath on the glass? I demanded. No, she said, I saw his face, its reflection, and here's the strange thing, should I tell you? I nodded my head, and she did so. I saw not his face, but my face, and when it clearly was my face, did it not turn into your face as you are now, as you were as a girl, as an infant, and as an infant I saw him in you, beckoning us all to come to him, as we do now in Zurich, gathering from all parts, getting here by hook or by crook, war or no war, boat and train and bicycle, ship and plane, some by the power of their two feet, or landing on stout wings, prompting a shout from your mother when she saw this miracle, she told us the man was an angel, qualifying her sense of awe by remembering that so too was Lucifer.

Tell her I laughed at that. Tell her it was funny. Tell her Father would have loved she thought of saying something comical as her heart was torn out of her. Tell her in my own way I made sure I saw what was happening in the room. Tell her I won't believe he's dead until I hear it from her own lips.

Tell her I want to see them move, saying, Your father has died.

Tell her. Tell her.

Tell her to come visit me.

CHAPTER FOUR

Father
Himself

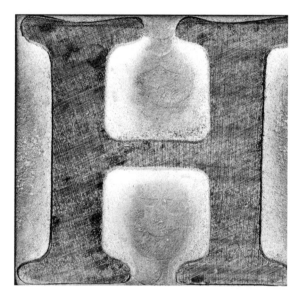

Bed

y son betrayed me. It is a family tradition. Didn't I do the same to my father?

I look at that boy and recognise nothing of myself about him. Might it be possible he is not mine at all? Is that why I take his treachery so easily? Has he escaped the curse defiling the lot of us? We hold our papas in such deepest and darkest contempt, we cannot wait to be rid of them lock, stock and baggage, ever ready with the match to light the bonfire that will greet the good news the old bastard is shaking off the mortal coil, he's finally doing a bunk, at long last he's breathing his bye-byes, and we'll leave him to finish that business without too much weeping and gnashing of teeth. Would that be the case when it comes to the pater? I would, if you look for confirmation here, direct your attention to my old boy and see what he might advise, after much cogitation and perplexity as to what is the proper fate every father, should he be hale and healthy, as I unquestionably was, or on the verge of kicking the bucket, as I now indisputably am.

Should I seek a second opinion on that diagnosis? To whom do I look to provide it? Friend or foe? Where might either be found? Would you credit I began my studies looking for a degree in medicine – was it in Paris or Dublin's fair city? I diagnosed myself with consumption, and given that I truly thought I had only days – or, at best, weeks, to live – well, I behaved with a most impressive display of restraint that, though I say it myself, could be taken as dignity. Such propriety I associate mostly with men of the cloth, my mother's dream for me since she rocked my cradle, but I could not oblige, nor indeed could I maintain the pose of the perfect gentleman. I engaged in a career serving the rhetorical arts and abandoned with equal fervour all thoughts of advancement in the Church.

Did that break Mama's heart? If it did, she made a most remarkable recovery, for she rarely spoke of my failure, or, as I prefer to call it, my betrayal, since as I told you I have passed that particular chalice onto my own issue, and he's drunk his fill from it with a drouth to match our own. Thus, he may well be mine, and shame on me for suggesting otherwise.

He is certainly sitting here, expecting me to croak. I

have reared him well never to think as his own the country which is my own, so I cannot be sure then if he knows that in the city which gave me birth there is a football stadium, Gaelic football, that is called Croke, and there young maidens go to die, deflowered on a day called the All Ireland Final, where they witness the human sacrifice of hundreds, thousands, tens of thousands, their blood stains the pitch red, and any who survive the studs of boots or the clash of sticks, the kicks in the face or the hand up the shorts, they are in their exhausted state allowed choose Queens of the May, those deemed suitable brides for boys who like a bit of beef on a woman. But the look of my son tells me, sure such carry on would kill him, so I'll leave him to his mother to make him a match as herself and myself never attempted, but fell across each other, as luck would have it.

Have we had much luck, the pair of us? All things remembered, might she seem as a bird of ill omen? Why did the Greeks believe the gods gave us instruction through the entrails of winged creatures? I heard tell of a woman years ago, somewhere in Rathgar, where my brood lived in one of our many flits, and she, they say, had tamed a magpie called Nanette to sit by her shoulder and whisper mysteries into her ear. The children believed Nanette was watching them and reporting back their misdemeanours committed out of human sight, but visible to the judging eye and condemning beak which blew the gaffe on all and sundry hoping to get away with any caper worth chancing. The woman herself fell for the illusion, fell so deeply she started to instruct Nanette on what was her Christian duty to report, unflinchingly, on the secrets and sins of her neighbours. Things came to a head when one man was accused of setting fire to a lady's undergarments drying on a washing line. He met this with derision and paid the price for his mockery.

She next charged him with killing his wife some years before, when that woman met her sudden end falling from a window in the Abbey Theatre, so overcome with revulsion at the poetry of a play that she raced with such speed out of the auditorium and into a piece of stained glass she mistook for a painting by Jack B. Yeats of a bog in Sligo. Inconsolable and all as he was at her loss, vowing as he did and keeping to that oath he would never set foot inside another den of such iniquity, he still could provoke the question in many minds, did she fall or did he push her? It all seemed somewhat far-fetched, the same woman was no innocent, certainly not one that would let the dialogue of a dramatist push her into thinking she could fly, for that's what it was claimed happened in some quarters. And how the hell would you mistake a painting for a window unless you were nearly blind?

It turns out she was – more than enough witnesses could testify to that – so the case was dropped and none dared bring it up again until Nanette let her suspicions be known. A foolish move on the magpie's part – she was found with her neck wrung, and her owner was as inconsolable as the man who lost his wife. He sympathised, of course, but she did not believe a word of that. Did he think her a complete eejit?

Were the Greeks, as I said a while back, complete eejits to set such store in what could best be described as prophecies? Such faith they had, that's no lie. If I were to rise from this bed and set myself the task of capturing a pigeon, dismembering it limb by limb, use the sharpest knife in the house to gut its chest open, what could I read contained therein? Would it tell me I will live or die? Would the gory patterns advise me to avoid my mother and run from my father? I tease out of its wings oil that smells of chrism, and with it, will I anoint my senses to purify as some priest in Delphi might to ready me for becoming – what? What am I becoming?

You are becoming your father's seed, bad son to your mother, harsh husband to a wife that loathes you, mocked by your son and daughter, blind to their laughter, paralysed on this bed, where you will soon meet your maker and he will not know you, he will not caress you, he will take hammer and tongs and crush you into embers, all this the divine bird chirps, should you care to listen. And I don't, I'm afraid. I have better things to do while I'm dying.

Pray tell me what they may be? I hear me ask of myself. Well, learn to cook, that's one of them. You cannot boil water, my ears tell my hands. But we are willing to learn, if given instruction, they reply in my defence. You could not peel a tangerine, my feet blame my fingers. The skin of that fruit is soft and delicate, I should enjoy touching – in fact, I do enjoy it, my thumbs answer, for in their defence they point out how often they have stripped the flesh bare and let me taste its lush nakedness. You could not bone a chicken with me, the sharpest knife in the house declares, you would cut your fingers, your feet, your hands, your ears, you are so clumsy, I am quite discomposed to find myself abused by your lack of grace.

I place the knife in a drawer to silence its attack, and should it care to listen, I tell in my defence the story of the duck stolen in Stephen's Green.

Our college fronted the Green, my alma mater. It had been founded, years before I attended, by a nun, Sister Henrietta Goodman. She had been born an Anglican in India and had grown to hate her religion. They say a toss of the coin decided her whether to become Buddhist or Catholic, and Rome won. The less kind of my countrymen intimated Sister Henry's own resemblance to the Buddha might have swayed her decision, but this is to underestimate the depth of her piety, the tenacity of her beliefs, and the sheer strength of her zeal that all be brought enchanted to the one true faith she embraced with such proof and vigour. A sign of this proof lay in her remarkable mission to convert to her religious philosophy the entire population of the town of Chelmsford in Essex, picked at random, but its men and women were well known for their lax, indeed perverse, attitude to all matters sexual. So successful was this Chelmsford Movement, as it was known, swarms of followers from every religious and intellectual tradition of Britain gathered in that most corrupt location to change their spiritual allegiance and be swayed by the teachings of this brilliant mind.

Not everyone was entirely supportive of the efforts of a woman who was, some declared, hell bent on sapping the moral fibre of the young men of the nation, scorning queen and empire perhaps to serve as minions in the armies of the Anti-Christ, as they called his holiness the pope. These calumnies wearied the poor woman to such an extent that when she heard the faith of the Irish was in dire need of reviving, didn't she turn her attention across the water and set out for Dublin, there to establish a university that would produce gentlemen such as ourselves who would do our island proud.

How did a simple nun pull off such a spectacular task? How does anyone succeed in doing anything in that lazy, accursed land of ours? Why, by working miracles, of course, and she did just that. Where was her first port of call when she had barely landed on this shore? Wasn't it Croke Park itself where a football match – or was it hurling? – had been held up while in full sway, when, as an act of retaliation for the murder of two diplomats, a battalion from the British army threatened players and spectators with rifles ready to blast them to kingdom come, unless the crowd reveal where the perpetrators of this evil act were hidden amongst them and agree to name their names so fit punishment could be visited upon them.

Nothing was forthcoming, and it seemed all would be caught in an unceasing stalemate, until the holy sister arrived and prayed that there be a resolution without more bloodshed, like good Christians. Well, it's said her prayers were heard, didn't the weapons of the soldiers – their guns – turn into lilies and sprout tall as trees, ascending suddenly from their hands and assuming the shape of the cross itself, falling in profusion on the mass grave where the handmaidens of the lord had suffered human sacrifice years before. Some expected these virgin martyrs would themselves rise and salute Sister Henrietta, but clearly she was not a woman who'd ask God for the impossible and drew the line at that.

This skill ensured the fame of her good self, even with the Protestant authorities ruling Dublin at that time. Give her what she craves, that was the consensus, for there were

many witnesses on many sides who swore she'd been working magic that day. Humour her for the love of fuck, or
who knows what havoc she'll unleash? What if she says she
wants a cathedral in the middle of Merrion Square? Is that
not over and above what we can afford? Wait and see, it was
advised, and indeed that was not her request.

No, she wanted a school, a university, a Catholic one, yes,
but she would call it after Victoria, the Queen's University,
Dublin. And so it took holy shape opposite Stephen's Green,
where Sister Henrietta Goodman founded her institution
to enlighten the young in the principles of moral forti-
tude and in the guidance of holy truths, where the sacraments could be obtained without fear or favour and where
learning might reflect the strictures of the commandments.
Strong drink was not encouraged in any room of the cold
establishment and, out of due respect for Sister Henry, no
woman was allowed to sully the chaste atmosphere of rev-
erent scholarship with their finery and fits of the vapours,
as the holy lady herself once remarked, jocundly perhaps.

She immediately corrected any sign of hilarity among
the men assembled. She herself had witnessed too many
such convulsions among her own sex to humour them

or to wish ever again to clean up their mess. She did not divulge where this behaviour occurred, but the rumour was that in India, Henry's mother spent her days in permanent hysterics, refusing to eat the spicy food or drink the boiled water, living entirely on a diet of the pages of bibles her unfortunate daughter had to wash in rum. The child interceded with the divinity for her mother's release from this manifestation of, shall we put it kindly, Scottish eccentricity – Mother was born a Lennox in Aberdeen – and received no reply to her fervent pleas for divine assistance, until her mother absconded with a Hindu priest devoted to the worship of Ganesh, the elephant god, leaving behind for her daughter nothing but a full set of riding clothes she might one day grow into and a recipe for a more than usually revolting Scottish broth, celebrating the humble neep as the emperor of vegetables.

After that, where next for the unfortunate child? The many arms of Kali might truly have drawn her, but she was, by temperament, more inclined to the serene Buddha, if she would grow entranced by the spells of Asia. She was, she claimed, saved from heathenism in a most strange manner. She heard the Buddha speak to her in a refined mockery of an Edinburgh accent, asking would she like to step out for a curry and a quick court. The maiden's disgust at the statue was quickly replaced with seething fury against her mother, for the girl could distinctly hear giggling from behind the sacred statue, and though she had never, ever in her life witnessed her mother laugh, the child was able to put two and two together and make four, realising there was only one tartan bastard would find this funny enough to scare the hell out of her, by leading her to believe a prophet was speaking through his stone image.

That instant decided her fate. If there was, she knew, one thing absolutely guaranteed to send the pack of Caledonian wolves that passed as her relations into paroxyms of rage, it would be that she'd decided to leap over the wall and join the other side who dug with the wrong foot and kissed the pope's fat arse while they were leaping, an act of physical dexterity she could demonstrate if called upon to do so. Rub the salt in the wound even deeper – she'd become a nun. Take the name of Henrietta as a homage to her grand-mother, a woman whose connection to the Orange Order was so tight she could peel the fruit of this name just by looking. That matron never travelled from her own house without carrying a lambeg drum, for who could know the day and hour when you might need one? And the last insult Henry added to their injury, she'd move to Ireland and live there, not among the beloved, saved brethren of the north – no, she'd go clodhopping down the south, lost in the array of Satan's hosts, she, who had been washed in the blood of martyrs and had sung with the choirs of penitents who once dared pick flowers on a Sunday, risking damnation. That's where she'd ply her works and receive due honour, while shaming all connected with her. Would she not stop and catch herself on?

As a matter of fact, she wouldn't.

She continued doing so much. The Catholic University was thriving. So as not to lose her, again they asked Sister Henrietta was there anything they could give her – anything she'd like? There weren't ready for her answer, because she replied, I'd like the ducks in Stephen's Green. Jesus, is she asking for Stephen's Green? A professor of chemistry misheard, being slightly deaf and a halfwit. Is there no end to the woman's notions about herself? Aren't they all the same, Jesuits? She's not a Jesuit, he was corrected, she's a nun, and she's only asking for the ducks, not the whole Green itself.

Why? What is it about the ducks?

I only ask they be protected, the woman clarified, that they be shown care and kindliness. Did you have one as a pet? she was asked. No, in my part of the world, such things were not encouraged, she enlightened them, dogs were for guarding homes, cats were to get rid of vermin, and horses always frightened me, although my mother doted on them and could get the most wild to do her bidding. My mother died, Henrietta shamelessly lied, having been thrown by her mount, jumping the most ferocious ditch, and she is buried in Kashmir. Maybe that's why I settle for smaller creatures and choose ducks as my darlings.

That term of affection was sufficient to ensure word got out that, not merely were the ducks to be protected, but that they were sacred as well, and must never be touched on pain of offending the nun and, perhaps, incurring her great wrath. So it was, with perverse undergraduate logic, a code of honour evolved that it became imperative when finals were at last completed, a duck must be slaughtered and served as centrepiece of the feast marking a farewell to the university.

Stories of their capture were legion. Copious amounts

of alcohol were downed to provide the Dutch courage necessary to pull off the exploit. The only time you could succeed, and not be identified, was in the dead of night. This aura of darkness added to the Satanic element of the creature's capture. No blessed object could dangle on any part of your anatomy, lest a divine light shine from it and give the game away. To lessen the sense of sacrilege and to pin some blame at least on the object of the prey, the duck to be captured would be called Judas.

The year we were party to the whole affair, more than a passing few of us were sick of this rigmarole, considering the preparation and execution an utter waste of valuable drinking time. I must admit I sided with the Carlow ruffian who said, Just catch the fucker and kill it, though I'm not risking it, I wouldn't thank you for duck meat as my dinner, its fatness turns my stomach. But it was the done thing to be man enough to follow tradition, and it might be in its strange way an insult to the old nun if we didn't make some fist of defying her.

The dead of night, we set out on our adventure. The gates of the Green locked, the streets of Dublin deserted, and us climbing the railings, no one got as much as a scratch, walking quietly towards the pond, one stalking the other, and not a murmur shared between us, for we knew what to do and how to do it quickly, since there was a boyo with us from Monaghan who had slaughtered fowl in their millions on his farm at Emyvale. We reached the pond's edge, and he was ready to wade in and catch the prize, but who did we see coming out of the shadows? The figure of the nun, waving a rosary beads, bidding us halt.

Jesus, the shock – we were near fainting, but the Monaghan hero was the first to recover, telling this apparition we meant no harm, for we had no notion who this could be, since her shape was certainly not that of Sister Hen. She turned her back to us and then pulled up the skirt of her habit, displaying her white buttocks to the chilly air.

Again the Monaghan man broke the silence, asking, Is that you, you Carlow fucker? I'd know that hairy arse anywhere. A guffaw greeted him, and we all copped on who indeed it was, the same messer who'd earlier declared he would have nothing to do with this lark. He also was brandishing not one but two ducks, on the grounds you could never have enough of a good thing.

Bad tempers faded rapidly back then, and we saw the

amusing side. Still, I was sorely tempted when he was having difficulty climbing back over the railing in his flowing dress to leave him dangling there. Luckily we got him down, for the next arrival on the scene was a policeman demanding to know what were we up to at this hour. Were you thinking of trespassing into Stephen's Green? he demanded. Not at all, we assured him. You wouldn't be after her ducks, the nun's? he warned us. Again, not at all, we repeated, and if you don't believe us, ask her. When he set eyes on the Carlow man begarbed in religious finery, it's fair to say from the look on his face, he did not know what hit him. Sister, he sputtered, what are you doing in this company? Aren't they the right little villains? the Carlow man declared, impersonating Sister Hen perfectly. Haven't they finished their exams, and now they're getting their bit of fun. Don't worry, constable, no harm done, they won't stray far with me watching over them.

He didn't disbelieve her. Nor did he want to know why she had two dead ducks in her fists. He was just another Irishman who believed a nun could not tell a lie. She was the same, my mother, Bridget. As was Bertha, when she was a girl in Galway. I know what put an end to her illusions, but Ma, did she go on believing in such innocence all the days of her existence? The days of her existence – why say that and not simply her life? Did she have one? And if not, did she turn her back on it? Did she reject it as being unworthy – herself being unworthy to do anything of note, anything that might impress on others she deserved a right to be seen and to be heard? Was she ever seen, was she ever heard, and if she were both, if she were either, then why can I not remember her face or her voice? Is that not a most damning comment on a son – he cannot summon a trace of his own mother? Will I be condemned to hell after this, my agony, not for all my sins, but for this omission of my mother from my memory?

How could this have happened? Why has it? I see in long procession the lines of my sisters and brothers. Each one blames me, pointing, that I insulted my mother, me, her first-born, her most beloved. She would have starved herself to give you the bite out of her mouth, they chide me. She barely had a change of clothes to dress herself, so that you would be warm, her that once was swathed in the finest furs, silks and laces, turned into a beggar maid so her lovely son would show the world he wanted for nothing, when it came to finery. Did she ever raise a hand to check you in all your fits and tantrums but calmly took you by the hand and caressed you, when the world was shouting what that brat needs is a hiding with his father's belt, and if the father isn't inclined to do so, then it's up to the mother to break the boy like the bad weed he's growing from, Christ between us and all harm. I do remember her, I declaim, for all to hear, I remember her, I have not forgotten her. Then why insist you do and leave yourself a laughing stock to anyone fool enough to listen?

I don't know, I admit, I never have known why I take such pleasure in denying my own. I have always done it. Preferred the company of those with whom I share no connection. Took great delight in making strange, particularly with the parents who reared me. When as an infant I wept, I calmed more at the touch of a stranger whom I'd never set eyes upon before, torturing the poor creature who gave me birth. What instinct made me hurt her? Or was I hating her? O mother forsaken, forgive your son. I was a child and did not know what I could do.

— *I think you did, my fine lad, I think you knew too well.*

Who's there? Who speaks, who is it? What voice is it

condemns me? Don't say that, now I'm dying, I have raised him from the dead, old companion, old chancer, old creator of my soul? Father? What do you want from me? Who let you loose inside this room? What do you bring? What havoc will you cause now – is it Christmas? What's that beneath your oxter, a football or a pudding, a plum pudding? Have you been kicking it round the city, taken it for a walk the length and breadth of Phoenix Park, sliced it for refreshments to feed your drinking cohorts and tried to patch it up again as if we could sit down and dine on it this holy day, rather than doing with it what it deserves, and what it deserves is playing it like a melodeon? If melodeon, it should play itself on its own accord, then give us a song, one of Balfe's, not that Gilbert and Sullivan tripe – the only time I feel sorry for the old queen is when they force Victoria to listen to their caterwauling they believe passes as music.

Father, sit down and eat your dinner.

He does so. And I say to my mother, without speaking, because she is adept at reading my lips, since we must never give away our secrets, why did you give him back the money? She gives the trace of a shrug, and makes the slightest move with her left hand, which reads, what else could I do? I am an honest woman. And if he had ever found out you chanced on that bundle of notes, and I'd taken a penny without telling him, would I have had the living of a dog? He would have had me hanged by the neck.

I nod, for she is right as she extracts from the measly turkey the lashings of stuffing that must make up this year the bulk of our festive fare. He suddenly starts to eye the pair of us, and we decide just to say nothing, for in this mood the least mumble provokes him, and every dish on the table, every dish in the house, could end up against the wall, so even if he's wondering why is this silence between us, there's better chance of a quiet time than if we were foolish enough to entertain him with a fight. I'd found the roll of notes on the stairs – how in Christ he came upon it we do not know nor do we want to – and I woke her to show them as she lay beside him in his stupor.

She nearly jumped out of her skin at the size of the amount. She took half and told me, as I expected she would, put the rest under your pillow, tell him that's all you discovered, when he wakes up and sees it all gone, I'll tell him. He will be so grateful it's not all missing he'll say nothing. She whispered, do you know what you've to do? And I nodded.

It all went as she said. He was nearly in tears searching for what he'd lost. He woke her and asked did she see it? He told her he was saving it for a pal and there would be hell to pay if it was not recovered. She said if he'd dropped it in the street, he could kiss the lot of it farewell. Maybe, though, he should ask the boy if he'd found anything.

I heard him race into my room up to my bed and pretended still to be sound asleep so he'd shake me awake and plead with me, hope against hope I'd found the loot. I looked at him, my father nearly crying, and I pulled the wad out from where I'd hidden it. He threw his arms about me and called me his darling son. He slipped me a pound note, or was it ten shillings? I asked him would he be giving some to my mother, and he told me she would not go short, but it had to be returned to the man who owned it. Who's he? I asked. Father Christmas, he joked and kissed my hair again, happy as Larry, happy as I'd ever seen him. And that morning I learned something about my father. Above all else, he loved money.

Then why had he so little of it? Because he made an art of squandering, and we suffered for this art. To please him,

I used to imagine how long we could all live on a loaf of bread, slicing it thinly, and when that was cut, dicing each morsel into maybe a single crumb, gathering it under my fingers, trying to make it last from the beginning of one month to the end, and when he saw how splendidly we could eke out our days and nights, how we could subsist on so very little, he would feel himself to be the finest provider in Dublin. He would smile on us and we would rejoice in our father's happiness.

Happy – our father, what a strange contact these words make – was the man ever anything but hell-bent on being forsaken by all he felt should love him most and who he did all in his power to make them hate him? What could have changed that? Who could have? Not my mother. If she'd put up more of a fight – if she had not withered – but she did all to please him, to serve her lord and master, and if she had to hide food to save it for us youngsters, then she would conceal it where she knew he'd find it, because he always did. What can I do against him? she would plead, he has only to open his mouth and I will obey, I have neither heart nor strength to resist him.

And neither did I, certainly not this Christmas night and

him rotten with whiskey. What's happened to that song, youngster? he roared, will you not gladden your papa's heart and humour the old fool when he asks you? I knew better than to play along and agree even in jest he was old or a fool, since truth be told he considered himself neither, but I struggled to find what should please him. If he disliked my choice, there was a chance all hell might break loose, and it may be wicked of me to admit I might be wanting such chaos. It could end the waiting for whatever might happen, depending on his mood. His fist hit the table – is the boy going to sing for me? I sang.

When other lips and other hearts
Their tales of love shall tell,
In language whose excess imparts
The power they feel so well:
There may, perhaps, in such a scene
Some recollection be
Of days that have as happy been,
And you'll remember me.

When coldness or deceit shall slight
The beauty now they prize,
And deem it but a faded light
Which beams within your eyes;
When hollow hearts shall wear a mask,
'Twill break your own to see:
In such a moment I but ask
That you'll remember me!
That you'll remember … remember me.

And now I start to weep for my father. Even on this, my
bed of death, I see him as young, a fine figure of a man,
raising his hand not to harm me but to caress, and if he
could within his power remove this agony that consumes
me, he would do so, giving for the relief of my suffering every penny in every pocket, in every lining where a
few bob might be the saving grace, having slipped through
a tear in a jacket sleeve and trouser pocket, falling to the
ground like manna from heaven to pay for the hair of the
dog or the one for the road, the best of the night − have
you heard about the widow woman suckled a sheep which
was said to be the sweetest mutton ever tasted and that's

not a word of a lie? Father, was there ever a word of a lie? Were you believed always and everywhere you travelled, whatever part of Dublin you chose to honour with your custom, never standing your round, for is that not the way of royalty around the world?

He had me convinced we sprang from kings and counts, archdukes and earls, and that our domain stretched as far as Donnybrook or the Liberties – penury there was as exotic to him, in the big house of his birth, as Bangkok or Baghdad. Though such grandeur might be lost, still he told stories of my strict old grandmother, a bad rip of the highest order, whose estate consisted of the foulest tenements in Dublin city, houses held together by dirt, their bricks breathing out consumption. That mean-spirited madam, she insisted on collecting in person the coinage of rents owed, holding an orange stuck with cloves to her nose, carrying a stout bag where the pence were collected.

She would stagger under the dead weight of these ill-gotten gains back to her mansion in Hatch Street, and there some little skivvy would pour boiling water into a tin bath, her job being to scald clean all the filthy shillings and dirty pence that were the foundation of our fortune.

Grandmother watched like a hawk the girl at her work in case the temptation to pocket a tanner proved too much. Not much chance of that occurring – the old lady had already in her clever head counted the exact amount should be steeping under the steam, washing it pure as her soul, praying at three Masses on Sunday in the church called Adam and Eve's. Yes, penny wise indeed, but was she pound foolish?

Who did she leave it to? Her darling son. What did he do with it? Let it fly from him, fast as shite from a shovel, for so himself declared. And why not, boys, why not? Wasn't there sport spending it, sport the old dear, his mother, could never have imagined, as she buried it down her drawers thinking it would rise with her, jangling on the Day of Judgement. Not a chance, Mother, whose lips never touched a drop, so didn't I make up for it? Did you attend as much as a single Mass said for the repose of her soul? he was challenged. Indeed and I did, he defended himself, one single Mass. Wasn't she holy herself in this life as a posse of Poor Clares? Will she spend a day in Purgatory?

I doubt it, for when she reached the Pearly Gates, St Peter would have found himself demoted and her given the keys of the kingdom, reigning over all lands. Such blasphemy! Wasn't that a dreadful way to be speaking of his dead mother, and her not cold in the clay? one cousin remarked. She added that she didn't think the Poor Clare Order moved in posses, as if they were cattle to be herded about the ranch of the Kingdom of God on earth. Let me clarify things here, my father explained, I would no more waste my time in the company of nuns than I would stick my hand in a bucket of dung. If that offends, I'm sorry, he added, and I give my apologies to the bucket. That cleared the house of them.

But soon they were gloating. You see, good luck couldn't come of it, such mocking and sneering – downright devil worship. Hadn't we lost the lot, or as much as meant they need never acknowledge us again? One bastard aunt paid a visit, seeking us out to prove to herself we were really penniless. Hardship makes even the mild less timorous, and my mother was working up to ask for a loan. But the flint-hearted relation hadn't held on to her First Communion money for nothing. She was not so much up to any possible request for charity but well ahead of it, for wasn't it just, at the very instant my mother was summoning all her courage to beg – that's what it was, no need to be polite, it was begging – that's precisely when our Lady Bountiful noticed she was not carrying her purse. Where could she have mislaid it?

Oh now, she remembers, in the kitchen at home, she can see it clear as daylight, she had just paid the butcher who'd called to settle his bill – the price of meat, we'll all soon be living on sausages – and there she'd put it down and quite forgotten it. As she had a few errands to run, would my mother be an absolute dear and loan her five shillings? She would send it back immediately.

Did my mother scream, how dare you? She did not. Did my mother tell that hag, who burns now in hell, the children in the house would go hungry if this money were borrowed? She did not. Did my mother give the miserable whore what she asked for? She did, and why? Because I hate her, my mother confessed, and I never knew the precise reason why, but I do now. Five shillings is a small price to pay to be certain, absolutely certain, that my contempt was correct. Mother knew she'd never get a smell of that do-re-mi again, but she would also never have to endure the stench of that barren bitch with her tonsils hanging out, starving for gossip and the bitter word, as my father described his relation.

Not that it stopped him approaching many others for whatever handouts he could garner. And my mother, she walked through Dublin, broken to the bone. She thanked the Sacred Heart I had brains to burn for winning scholarships and prizes that at times kept us fed. If I told my wife these stories, she'd laugh in my face, reminding me of what want was really like, no Dublin jackeen could have a notion of that, you needed to hail, as she and all her breed did, from the famished West of Ireland. She claimed a second cousin had, years before, married into a crowd that survived for seven months once upon a time on a diet of stones stolen from a wall in the Aran Islands, ground down into a paste, mixed with salt, pepper and water, with no more taste than grass.

Where did they get the pepper? I asked her. If they were that destitute, how come they had access to such a luxury? It was given to them, she ascertained, and they were thankful for the kindness, not inclined to insult those generous enough to comfort. If the best that shower could rise to was a shake of pepper, I maintained, then their heads deserved to be chopped off and eaten for supper. Aren't you the clever fellow? she jeered. I know for a fact they were given a whole drum of pepper and it made the soup more than a little palatable. Well, were that the case, I observed, they might have tried to swallow the slabs of the stone wall itself, to stop them indulging over much on its harshness, delicious and all as it might be. Jesus, woman, do you ever listen to yourself? I queried of her. There's times you'd sicken a goat.

We bred goats, you know, once upon a time, she remembered, God between us and all harm, but they're disagreeable creatures. I used to spend the summer months living on the slopes of Nephin mountain, working as a goat herder with my uncle, Phonsie, who was a shepherd and never married, so devoted was he to his flock.

You're a confounded liar, I let her know, you'd no more touch a goat than you would a wasp. Where do your stories spring from?

Well may you ask, she snapped back at me, and well may you answer, for aren't you the expert on this matter? Isn't my head turned trying to keep up with the ins and outs of all your flying fucks of what happens next and where is this all going? Aren't you the one constantly leaving me lost as to what is and what is not, according to your imagination? Is my son capable of leaving the house without a bottle somewhere on his person? Is my daughter falling asunder? What kind of mad yahoos do they attract? A woman who doesn't know if it's morning, noon or night? A Protestant Sammy who doesn't wash himself and smells like a fishing boat and its contents? I wouldn't be breaking my neck paying for either wedding, if one ever is to happen by some miracle. But you ask me, where do my stories spring from? I'll answer you – they're from my life, unless you know differently. Do you?

I didn't, so I let it rest, though I had a good idea what was coming next, and it would touch on my daughter, Beatrice. When was the last time you entered a church door? Bertha wanted to know. But I was ready for her and, quick as lightning, I replied, I did stray into a synagogue not that long ago. Does that qualify? It does in my book, I let her know, just to prod her. You'll be watched by all the enemies of Zion, she warned me, and there seems no shortage of those boyos in this day and age. Maybe it's an honour, I replied, to be so watched. Tell me that the next time you're stuffing your face with bacon and cabbage, she hissed. I'll save you the cabbage, I offered her, you can wear it instead of lipstick. What was it I was called – by your mother or by your aunt – was it a painted hussy? Bertha asked, or was I just country cute, as they termed me? You should know, you carried the story with you. And I wonder what they'd say if the same ladies got a glimpse of our daughter in all her glory. What do you think would be their response?

I would not rise to this, I kept my mouth shut. Do you think they'd be charmed? she continued. What would they make of her? Would they talk to her? What do you think they'd advise? Would they believe she needed a priest or a doctor? Haven't you years ago trotted her out to all the mental homes and mind readers in Switzerland? Have they told us anything we don't already know? Didn't one say it all came down to dreams, her madness, and it was yours, not her own, that were troubling her? How can that happen? How have you entered her brain like that? What kind of badness – and badness it is – have you been stirring to succeed in pulling off such a strange trick, when it's protecting the poor fool you should be, not leading her even more astray, giving her access to your musing and all its meandering. What are you at? Why don't you stop it? Why don't you give in? Me, I'd try anything to right what's wrong with her.

Why won't you? she entreats. Why will you not take her to Mass? Why can we not ask a priest for help?

She knows my answer. She cries a bit but recovers herself. So you won't lower yourself, she repeats. But if I want to introduce my daughter to the powers of Satan, you will not stop me. Well, that's a big help, she nods, a great help indeed, thank you, I'll bear your advice in mind. Good Christ, I think you're enjoying this, seeing me in such a state, and you as serene as she is. What else did he say, the Geneva doctor, if doctor he is? Did he tell you how she hates me? Hates her brother? Did he tell you she is doing what her father bids her? No answer to that, have you? That certainly shook you. Do you think I do not know your little arrangement? Once it was all right me reading your books and following whatever made head or tail as you decreed it should be, and I swallowed this to make some fist of what kind of man you are, but that had to stop when she took control of the reins and led your horse to water on what under Jesus was fabricated by the pair of you. I'm not saying you touched her where you shouldn't – her tits, her woman, her arse, they went unmolested, although life might be a lot simpler if that were not the case.

No, you went deeper, and you didn't want to go alone. Did you know the destruction you were weaving? Did you know there might come a time she would not come back? She was your mind run riot, never knowing when to halt. You're being very quiet – but tell me, am I right or am I wrong?

Are you ever wrong? I ask her. Am I ever right? she corrects me. But is your brain not frazzled? I want to know. Worn down, not what it was, spinning on its axis. As it is this day while I am dying, daring my wife to challenge that.

She does so with tears, tears of sorrow, of recrimination, all against herself. Our son enters and tries to embrace her, but she turns away. Where have you been? she asks him, how was I to manage here on my own? What if something happened?

I went for a walk to the graveyard, he tells her, but she stops him, saying such talk could hasten the hour, it was unlucky. And what about my sister? he asks. What about her? she demands. What good can she do? He turns directly to his mother. Will we try to get her word? She should at least know. Should we try to bring her here?

Are you as insane as she is? My wife now is furious. How do we get her from France across the Swiss border? And if we could arrange that miracle, what would we do with her? Could you nurse her? I certainly could not, she has the strength of a horse when the wildness is on her. It would take a team of six male nurses to hold her when she's awry, and she is always now awry, isn't she?

She sees he is crying, she pats him on the shoulder, she says quietly, we did what we could, we saved her from herself.

No, you saved her from myself, that is what you mean, isn't it, Bertha? How wise women are when they are jealous. That is when they see things most clearly. When their suspicions let them smell the workings of all that's sour, that's rancid in the human heart. Did I desire my daughter? As she danced, did I out-Herod Herod? But what if I had such eyes, only for my son? What then would my wife say? Might she then admit I was indeed her rival for his affections? If I am to stand accused in some mean or manner of incestuous thought, why should such a charge enter her head against me, if it had not already been present in her longing for our boy, as beautiful in his way as the sister he rivals? Were I to choose on which to lay loving hands, would my wife insist on removing such choice as her way of being in sole control of what fate could befall this strange family?

Or is it so strange? What have I done to incur divine wrath? Is a thought a deed? An image, an action? My little ones, they run from me as if I would besmirch them, but I am an old man, paralysed by illness, his body broken by ague, his blood a weary stream running dry of tributaries. What rain falls from these bones is poor stuff indeed, perhaps a noxious mixture to poison carnations, the rose and sunflower, the glories of our garden that once did dazzle, sending all our swains and their Sylvias into each other's arms, swearing eternal bondage, embracing their chains of beaten gold and enchanting silver, loosened from the very bowels of the moon, that if I could but release that matter from me, I might get up from this bed and stretch out my legs, my arms, my feet, my fingers, my toes. Let the eagles of Zeus carry me, feast on me, his Ganymede, an offering to my father, my heavenly father, that he can fuck me as he likes if that be his pleasure, as it was not my pleasure with son nor daughter, and for this filthy chastity, I am punished with death. There is no pleasing some.

Marcel Proust there was no pleasing that time I met him. He would be intent on talking cricket, a subject not to my liking, yet meat and drink to my daughter's young admirer, who hailed from Foxrock and played the game for Ireland, but as this bed I lie on could also play cricket for Ireland, I counted it, as he to his credit did, a small achievement.

Not so Proust who proved himself, in the intricacy of their conversation on the topic, to be quite the expert on the odd and suggestive quality of the sport. Why this fascination? I inquired. He replied, their whites, the cricket whites, they transform the roughest beasts into cherubim. The colour obsessed him, and every recipe devised in his masterpiece Cooking for Phantoms, displayed through its multiple volumes that passion. Above all, he prided himself on his creation of a cheese sandwich, the gentlest brie, so pure its milk might never have touched a cow's tit, served toasted, not on a slice a bread, but on a tarot card, the choice of whichever image from the pack specified the fate this greatest of chefs believed in store for his hungry guest.

My cricket-loving young friend was exceptionally adept in all the arts of necromancy, so this combination of expertise made him a more than irresistible intrigue for the older man. I do not, naturally, know, nor, if I did, would I reveal, should there be any truth in the rumour that one of these gentlemen made a salacious move on the other, only to be rebuffed in no uncertain manner. It is said by many, but not myself, that the root of bad feeling between me and the French cook dates from this, since the young Irishman is reputed to have audibly asserted if he were now or ever in the future inclined to caressing another cock I would be the object of his wandering hands, and not the Gallic groin of my rival.

Rival he must be called, despite the narrow scope of his subject, because there is no denying the brilliance, and, may I say so, even if such a description might lighten his widely admired sombreness, the sheer buoyancy of his prose – my wife also swears by his poached eggs paprika, as she informed him, a touch too loudly, on the only occasion they met. She was rewarded for the compliment with a look on the face of the great man she described as a slapped arse. I pity the poor woman has to warm his sheets in the winter, she remarked. He is not married, I informed her, but his housekeeper is devoted. She's welcome to him, she observed – Jesus, for a man so steeped in the pleasures to be savoured from the fruits of the earth and the sea, isn't it an awful pity he can't bring himself to be pleasant and speak civilly to your neighbour sitting politely at the table near you? Was he never taught manners maketh the man? And they cost nothing, though I say it myself. Still, you have to admire a mind that tells you to smear a touch of tarragon mustard on your strawberries. From where did he come up with that?

She still declined to let Proust know her esteem, and so he passed all too quickly, or not quickly enough, out of our circle. To his dying day, I hear he spoke slightingly against us – too Irish to be civilised or some such rot.

Mind you, he could be right. Are we that lacking in finesse? In savoir vivre? Well, you might say I should come up with an answer there, for if any man stands accused of pushing the boat out into the wild ocean of wine, women and song, might it be my good self and the sewers of books with which I did pollute the minds of the young, the old, those in between, devout schoolgirls divesting themselves of black woollen stockings, reciting the ins and outs, the why and wherefores of my dirty old books, fit only to be repeated by giggling boys, hiding the pages they were reading in hands they had covered with cream of their own churning, swearing to good God and his mother in heaven they would never, ever tell their female relations, from oldest to youngest, how they might scandalise these gentle womenfolk by admitting they had read my words, written on paper best used in a lavatory for a purpose I was only too keen to celebrate?

And now, look where such dirty talk has landed me. Do you see how I dumped my dose scribbling this filth, and this is how I fare in the end – a living corpse stretched on a single bed, not so much deserted or disowned by his nearest and dearest as reduced in my stupor to realising that all of them, wife, son, daughter, each in their unique way, is as insane as the other, and in their rare moments of clarity, the same trio see me as the source of their madness. Who have I to blame? Well, if I pushed my luck, I could point the finger at Marcel, say my head was turned completely by his queer attentions, but nobody would buy that, especially myself. I could look closer home. Name my own mother and father. But I'm stopped in my reveries of days long gone by what happens next.

It is my son, Archie, and he's shaking me. If I could hear, he would be screeching into my deaf ears to open my blind eyes. To see himself and his mother. They beg me not to leave them, for they do not know what will become of them, should I no longer be alive to let my reputation as a writer save them from the forces of darkness overrunning all of Europe. If I could see, I would bear witness to his mother, calmly removing his hands from my fragile body before he shakes apart my bones and sockets, tendons and sinews, their eccentric form bearing next to no correspondence to the normal configurations of the human skeleton, transforming me into – say what? A hyena or a zebra, an exotic creature of the wilds, now trapped inside my sorry skin, longing to be freed by him, my boy, trying in his most useless way to stop me dying?

It will not work and he knows it, but does it stop him trying to save me? If I could talk, I would be able to advise the young blighter there is no hope for us in this earth we are destined to wander, seeking salvation that always lies beyond us, though we may have feasted and dined ourselves silly on the dreams and nightmares of mankind. What long annals they could fill, and here I swear by all that is ignoble and incriminating I'll tell my favourite.

I was in a city, somewhat like Dublin, in a building, a rather grand edifice, resembling a castle. You might imagine I would find myself uncomfortable in this spacious domain. The reverse is true. I walked from room to room in that splendid mansion, and nothing, nowhere seemed unfamiliar. I did notice a clock, a particular clock, on a bare mantelpiece that must have been dazzling white in its day but now showed signs that time was staining it. On the face of the clock there was a winged horse, Pegasus, I'm sure, and if I remember correctly, his legs were the minute and second hands, both of which had stopped, or is it just in dreams everything stops or conforms to a motion of its own making?

The next I knew the horse beckoned me inside the glass, but I resisted, shaking my head, whereupon without the least ado, he beat his wings and stood before me in this singular location, neighing loudly, stamping his hoofs until I would mount his back and surrender to the whip of his will, taking me where he chanced to fly. The ceilings of this castle, covered with all the constellations in heaven, they opened to allow us safe passage upward, and so it was that I became a cavalry man among the stars, perched, terrified, on the back of this most snarling steed, growing even more fearful, though he came only from dreams, as I well knew, but could not shake sleep from me.

Why had I been given access to this crazed passage between heaven and earth? Was it to see my city as no human creature ever had before? And what use should I make of this precious knowledge steeping into my mind's eye? What was sprawled beneath me? Some wonderful fabric never before cut from a bolt of silk that had lapped all the colours Marco Polo brought from Cathay? What was painted on it? The streets and their alleys, the green avenues and gardens, the lanes and squares, the tenements and towers, the sea fed by rivers, the chapels and pagodas, the gutter of its gossip all waiting to be sipped by me like mother's ruin, most divine delirium.

How long were we hovering in that air which smelt – I now recall – so strangely of peaches, peeling themselves of flesh, perfumed, desirable, every blind bit of it. Let me have a bite – let me have two – let me devour the lot, stones and all, no bother – I can crack whatever's put in front of me, and if it chokes, it won't be for lack of trying to swallow all in one gulp, as a hungry man should do, shouldn't he?

Was I always starving, would you say? Did I have a thirst like the Sahara desert? That is what I feel this dying day – a want of river the Liffey could not satisfy. A hole in my belly bigger than the Gresham Hotel. I promised you, my darling, we'd stay a night there, do you remember? Looking up at the lit windows, who could not imagine flopping down on a soft feather bed beneath us, our hands removing skirt and trousers, shaking bedspreads and feeling pillows, the taste of the best champagne tripping us into each other's arms, smelling the two of us of all the lavender ever grown on the island of Ireland, and never, ever letting each other go for love nor money, for richer, for poorer, for health or sickness. No, no talk of ailments. No brooding on what's broken and can't be mended, this night we're in the Gresham, or as near it as we'll ever be, clap hands and watch it all appear, the trays laden with the best of turkeys and ham, goose, buttered cabbage, cream to beat the band. Your wish is their command in this grand hotel.

But will they let a country bumpkin in, you ask, not

knowing in their opinion her arse from her elbow? Would you bother entering, my darling, if they said yes? Who was it brought home to you that you were not fit to skivvy there, let alone stay? What a shower of snobs, and what were they but bloody servants, washing dirt off the spuds? Beggars on horseback, surely, and you were ever less than a beggar in that establishment, you declare, vowing never to step over its threshold, their cruelty towards you breaking your heart for one great reason. Will I tell what? As a girl, you dared to hope when you got married, the breakfast would be there in the Gresham. A beautiful frock, and soft shoes, and a veil whose train stretched the whole length of Ireland from east to west, to your house in Galway, across the Bog of Allen, not a single mark of dirt touching it, and you as pure, as beautiful as your bridal gown, wrapping it around every nook and cranny, every brick of the hotel where you invited everybody – yes, everybody – you'd ever met in your whole life to be your most welcome guest on this most happy of days.

Day you always wanted. And which I barely gave you. Should I do so now, on the night I'm dying? What is it I could ask you?

Will you marry me?

Why should you? What have I to offer? Too late for the ring, too late to shell out for whatever the band of gold sets a man back. So what else instead?

For your hand would you take a story? Will you settle for that?

If so, here's mine —

CHAPTER FIVE

The Woodcutter and His Family

ow long ago was it there lived a man, a woodcutter, near a forest not that far distant from hereabouts? If I had a clock on the mantelpiece or a calendar facing the clock, I could tell you exactly, but since neither such contraption now exists, being smashed with the mirror that brought us all bad luck, a fine silver mirror that you'd swear was so haughty in its silence – it could buy and sell you as well as answer back that it was fairest of them all – there is little way of pinpointing when he graced these parts. We were ruled then by ogres, but they had long before fallen into a deep, deep slumber from which there seems to be no awakening, since they are still sleeping to their heart's content in some corner of the country that nobody can now locate, and why should any do so? We are all inclined to let them dream on. Let us forget them in their terror and cruelty.

But it's true he is still remembered, the woodcutter. One vague rumour persists he worked as a hangman for some despot or other in China, but that can be ignored. You can be certain he'd never set foot upon a boat in his life, so how could he have reached Asia? On foot? By bike? Driving a van or lorry? No, he put his trust always and ever in Shank's mare, swearing it the only safe way a body could get about. And in his travels he did cover a fair distance, that is why many do recall him quite clearly, some describing a fine figure of a man, nearly six foot tall but with bad eyes that squinted. Others swear he was stooped, badly stooped, almost a hunchback. I am myself certain about this disfigurement, though no one else goes that far. But almost to a man and woman, they agree with me he had a beautiful singing voice, the sweetest, lightest tenor, with which he entertained all and sundry while he was working, serenading them with 'Under the Greenwood Tree':

> Under the greenwood tree
> Who loves to lie with me
> And turn his merry note
> Unto the sweet bird's throat,
> Come hither, come hither, come hither:
> Here shall he see
> No enemy
> But winter and rough weather.

Who doth ambition shun
And loves to lie in the sun,
Seeking the food he eats
And pleased with what he gets,
Come hither, come hither, come hither:
Here shall he see
No enemy
But winter and rough weather.

Others maintain this is malarkey – he was an Irishman through and through, the woodcutter. Would he be caught dead carousing with this song, a blast from England, the old enemy's past? But he had no quarrel with the English, many maintain – in fact if you listened carefully to his voice, could you not detect a decided touch of London buried in his brogue, as if the same boy had spent a fair few days settled there, doing what, nobody had discerned, and if they had, they weren't telling? So there you have it. People argue over what he did and who he was. Men claim that this good fellow, ancient as he was – old as the hills when I first knew him, my father claims – this shadow of a shadow, he could still toil for days at a time, running into weeks, without much rest for the luxury of sleep and sustenance. Women, large and small, insisted he was, contrary to the opinion of their male folk, a rather handsome and vigorous chap, if a little withdrawn and disinclined to mix, with a healthy head of red hair. Others contradicted that, countering it was jet black, and one nervous lady dared to venture that his hair was blue as the sky. She had watched him once washing it in a river, and hadn't the water itself turned cobalt after he'd dipped his head in, giving his curls a shade of azure when they were clean and dripping wet, staining his face as if it bore the marks of a farmer's sheep. When she dared to ask him why it was such an unusual colour – could it be hereditary? – he looked at her as if there was nothing irregular in the whole business and kept his mouth shut, not giving her the pleasure of an answer. She knew better than to interrogate further.

Such is the way we can see each other, none of us agreeing, but all the ladies declared that it was not the scale of his labours that they marvelled at, but rather the precision, indeed the beauty of his carving, when he had a mind to do it. This exquisite decoration on every item of his work depicting the strangest combinations of creatures you could ever imagine, telling stories of women, men and gods, all creating chaos and confusion, holding each other down in positions impossible to repeat – this is what should be given pride of place in all discussion centred on him, and let all bitter word cease.

Try telling that to the children, though. They were frightened of his fierce eyes. He always seemed to scowl at them for no reason under the sun, and at times when they looked at his cross face, his redness seemed to burn them. A few of the rougher ones bravely spun the story that he barked at them. Indeed, there was serious word in some schools he might bite you with his black teeth, sinking them into the white calf beneath your trouser leg and crippling you for ages, if you ventured too near the smelly, sweaty woodcutter and him slaving away, sending bits of rough bark in all directions.

One lad wet himself with fear, just listening to tales about the woodcutter in the playground, and everybody saw the big stain. They smelt it too. The poor boy became a laughing stock, and would have earned a nickname of Pissabed for years to come, had his granny not died suddenly and so common sympathy saved him from shame, but the night before his wedding years later didn't some fine wag leave outside his door a bunch of dandelions just to let him rest assured not everyone forgot how he'd lost control of his bladder and gave them all a laugh, best of luck to him and his blushing bride. Whoever did this, to their credit still and all, they also must have been one of many who were constantly fetching the woodcutter sweet tea and fancy bread a neighbour asked them to deliver, but that gift of grub was no guarantee they would be spared his rough greeting to clear out of his sight or he'd chop them into kindling. Well, that's a threat one very nervous fellow swore he'd heard, but none could confirm it.

No, nobody else would back that up, but everyone knew it was far safer when the woodcutter kept his counsel, or if he only said that too little sugar had been stirred into his cup, or he'd point out how few raisins found their way into his buttered slice of treacle scone, yellow and brown in his browner hand, smelling of wind and weather no scrubbing could eradicate, or wash away entirely. Yet he was a cleanly man, who could dispute that? Immaculate on a Sabbath day, he was, when he attended neither church nor chapel. But it was best, if you were attending on him, that he'd simply point to where on the ground they should put his food and drink, leaving him to grunt any thanks he felt should be offered.

No one ever saw him chewing a bite in his mouth. He had a horror clearly of that being witnessed, it was suggested. Why? Had he some way of swallowing – some way of digesting, even of cutting his meat that he wanted none to know about? That it was his business and only his, maybe summoning spirits from the earth to protect him from poisoning? Had he been scalded with his mother's milk, the woodcutter? Did that give him some kind of fear of food, a fear no royal taster, had he the money to pay such a lackey, would remove? Did he take no relish in what was put before him on the table, feel no surge of want for what was lying on his neighbour's and not his own plate, never stretch his fork out and grab a tasty morsel before anyone else got their claws on it? What was bred in the bone that taught him greed was the least effective of all human vices? Some knowledge that once you satisfied yourself, all that could happen next was to want more? Sate yourself again? Did he know all these things? No one could tell.

He did, however, cough up for what was put before him.

Watch him carefully, and it was never quite as easy as you and I might find it, doling out when we need to pay the piper. There was a way he had, and only he had, of handling money. It was not as if he were cheating, far be it from me to accuse him of that. That is not now, nor would it ever be, my intention, but it's fair to say there was a slyness to the whole paraphernalia of settling the bills. What do I mean by that? Well, he didn't so much put his hand in his pockets to extract the monies owed but seemed to breathe coins out of the air, silver, copper, as if he was conjuring them, bright and newly minted, you might say, untouched till now. So he handed over what was owed, asking and expecting no questions, the biggest of which was for us, of course, had he anyone belonging to him?

If he did, no one was saying, and neither was he. There were, as always, rumours, but we had learned not to credit them. Weren't there enough spread about ourselves and not a glimmer of truth to be found in any? We were reputed to be master brewers, our beer exclusively served to the gentry, but all we did was drink the stuff in such copious quantities that had we the licence to make it, I do swear we might be the richest family in the land. No, we learned to swallow tall stories with a large packet of Saxa salt. Take the one about the witch who was supposed to have stolen him to be her husband, while he was innocently planting bluebells in a convent garden. Her ugliness was said to have put him under a trance, her face as pitted as if it had been carved from honeycomb or from red spuds, and she had a wart as big as a pear on her nose. To add insult to injury, it was claimed she had three nipples, but I'll stop there and ask the only question that needs answering, was he a husband in the first place? One pretty girl smirked, who would take him? As far as such a suitor was concerned, she had her hand safely glued to her ha'penny.

Then there came an evening, long and bright, when the word emerged that he was, as they say, spoken for. I can no more give you the exact time and place where he made this revelation than I can identify the smart arse who had the brilliant idea of slipping a sup of Bushmills into the scalding sweet tea he liked to down in one go, priding himself on the power of his swallow.

The woodcutter tasted nothing strange, and he was too innocent a creature to realise what change had crept upon him. Well, this drop of the jar, didn't it loosen his tongue –

loosen it a little, but enough to make sure the craic would
be ninety if you could get this geezer more ancient than
Noah's Ark to wheeze out every secret buried in his bones
and blood and spill the beans about himself since – who
knows? – there might be a bob or two hidden where he
nested, not trusting banks nor shares, or what have you.
Thus it came to pass one morning in July, the sun beating
down, splitting the stones, the ould fellow's throat dry as a
Welsh dresser, his tea was so strongly laced he was more
than three sheets to the wind and though not quite drunk
as a skunk, didn't he tell the nosy parker of a neighbour
indeed he was married, and it was to the forest.

When the world and its wife caught wind of this piece of
news, glee and merriment at the poor fool's expense were
the order of the day. There were some who sympathised,
though. For years it was believed among a few who had
carpenters in the family that working with timber, in some
cases, it could perplex the brain. Coarser folk wondered if
he might be suffering from splinters stuck in a most tender
part of his anatomy, acquired when he was on the job with
a sycamore? Another wag expressed his opinion no chair
nor table in any house would be safe from his amorous

intentions. A third revealed he was quite determined to make an honest woman out of a garden gate that had been in his possession for years, swinging to and fro, it was time to stop her gallop and stand by her at the altar. A local clergyman got wind of this threat, and the following week preached a sermon denouncing the end of marriage and civilised family life, if such perversities as this proposed alliance between a man and a piece of garden furniture were allowed. There would be no chance of such an outrage occurring in his church, he assured his parishioners, many of whom shifted uncomfortably in their pews, betraying perhaps the beginnings of bad thoughts that, without the priest's assistance, might never have troubled them.

For some reason, the young took a particular pity on the woodcutter. One girl left a note pinned to a tree in a pink envelope she got in a Christmas stationery set, warning him of this mission to discredit him. He never got it. If he did, he gave no sign, not even bidding her the time of day, passing her. So she soon forgot about him, a stranger who was married to a forest.

It was true though, for among his kith and kin, this was the done thing. A custom in which his breed believed, a breed where boys could take up to nine years – years, I said – before they were fit and ready to leave the womb and leap, weeping, into the arms of their utterly exhausted mothers. These poor women suffered from no maternal deficiencies, but can you blame them if they were utterly delighted, certainly putting up no resistance, when the male infants were left to shelter under and indeed suckle from a chosen tree – silver birch or oak, larch or elm, willow tree and rowan? From this solid presence in the soil stretching to infinity down its trunk and its roots buried securely under the ground, the male child drew strength, as you would from father or mother.

He must revere the tree. Worship it even. Never let harm come upon its head. Pray to it, if he was of a mind to imagine prayers could be heard. Defend it – be its champion, its warrior, whatever the elements of the earth or the waves of the sea might hurl against it. For many years, if necessary, he must prove his mettle doing this. Then would come the terrible test – the ordeal he must endure without complaint. From all the trees waiting in the forest for the killer blow, the one he lay under, the chosen branches, that must be the first one he would fell, weeping that it was no more, slain by his cruel hand, both patricide and matricide.

For such an act of unspeakable, inexplicable violence, there would be only one punishment. He must prostrate himself before the whole forest and all the creatures living within it. Begging mercy, he would let the trees whom he had defiled choose a bride for him. They left him to wait the customary period of a year and a day – if he made his mother wait nine years in the womb, he can bloody wait for us, they figured – until he heard their voices whisper through the leaves where he would find her. She was waiting under the chopped branches of that tree now fallen but sacred to his destiny.

Were she asleep, under no circumstances was he to waken her, on pain of death, with a kiss. Linger instead for her eyes to open. He found her precisely where she was meant to be found. Her lids remained closed for what seemed eternity. Yet they did reveal themselves, and he asked her what her wedding gift should be. She greeted this request with silence. Still, he could hear the music of the forest, played through the mouths of its inhabitants, flesh, fish and fowl. Their song was low, but quite distinct. It seemed to carry within all the refrains and burdens, the ballads and rhythms of his life and its sorrows, illuminating him with their depth and number, more than he had ever confronted, bringing no peace but something else past understanding, making his lips move, yet neither word nor melody emitted from them, only a desire to do as she would have him. She read that in his face and then responded to him. She said, I want a city – build me a city.

What kind of city? A city more secretive than Ur of the Chaldees, she responded, with its shrieks of human sacrifice, tearing the heart out of a body made to listen to that suffering, longing for Abraham, our father, to heal it and make terror go away. A city more storied than Illium and all the towers of Troy, falling on its womenfolk now enslaved by Greeks, stilling the troubled mind of Queen Hecuba, broken by great pain, searching for her Priam, howling like a mad dog who has lost her pups, drowned before her eyes, yelping for their mother, swearing vengeance. A city more delicate than Kyoto, its temples cut from rice paper, its streets a swarm of flowers left before its pagodas, requesting the Shintu gods to spare Japan and all its islands, to bless the divine wind that will protect its ships and sailors from the vengeance of eagles and the bolts of lightning, lightning that is itself the gift of those same divinities, their blessings, which will destroy as much as they will desecrate all who worship. A city more dirty than Dublin, if that's all you can rise to. But for Christ's sake, spare us Cork and all its environs. Do that at least for me, she pleaded.

Then he wondered, where shall I build it? In the forest – out of the forest, she ordered. And he obeyed.

He did construct for her a palace of great beauty and awe, crafting his skill with miraculous speed, since only when it was complete would she lie with him. He did not question her insistence nor fear her reluctance, but he did wonder what she was getting up to all day when she would disappear from his sight. He determined to find out and, when he asked, received the answer she was learning the language of the forest, its multitudes of grammars, its skeletons of syntax, its teeming womb of metaphors and similes, the ins and outs of irony, the lies of ambiguity, preparing herself for the day she would pass on such excellent knowledge to their young, as if what she acquired by instinct would transform itself into their intelligence.

Then it was ready, this glorious site. Soon she gave birth to sons and daughters that they might go forth and multiply to populate the gold dwellings and silver dens of splendid iniquity in this land. She had instilled in each of her young the value of frugal necessity and thrift, but they paid little heed, preferring to avail of their father's plenty. They praised to the skies the beauty and daring of his handiwork. This pleased him, as it did beyond measure his wife, reigning here jointly with him in this, their paradise, which, in their contentment, she had bestowed on their brood of sturdy lads and comely maidens. They wasted all they owned, but they did love their father, the woodcutter. Well, they loved him for a time. Then they grew sick in their souls of the smell of timber.

When can we leave here? his eldest son demanded one day. I am tired of this place. Where else is there, his daughters longed to know, that we may see more marvels? How long must you cage us? They clamoured to discover what he would answer. And it did not stop, morning, noon nor night, wanting to be clear from home, as if they were bound by chains cut from beaten gold, or their fetters were carved from gorgeous ivory. They had wearied of the forest and all it could provide for them, merely by asking, and all was fetched immediately for their delight.

But nothing did delight in the end. Their desires turned now to creatures of the forest, breeding with them, giving birth to centaurs and to satyrs, gentle beings whom their human parents disowned, loved only by the goats and horses that knew them as their own, forgiving the filthy strain that linked them to our species, we who cursed them for resembling ourselves in their imperfect shape. And so the heartless sons and daughters grew more and more discontent.

How long, they repeated, how long are we to be held here? When will we shake the dust of this place from the soles of our feet?

When we die, their parents smiled.

And after that, what shall we do? And when will you—

Die? When you leave us.

Did that satisfy them? It was said not. A son, in the business of worshipping fire, devised rites and rituals that might empower him, should any believe him capable of unleashing chaos. Perhaps he did succeed – one night lightning struck the stump of that tree where beneath its broken branches the mother once dozed, waiting to be awakened by their father.

Was it the eldest son? The very same, many swear. From

its ashes he'd learned the mysteries of fire. He even went so far as to believe as an infant he'd sprung intact from within a burning bush. Nobody took the trouble to dissuade him. Anyway, all he did was breathe carefully upon a pile of cinders, let the sparks mesh, and then relish the flames now ascending, blazing the city in the forest.

Thus was his father's, the woodcutter's, handiwork turned to red dust. His mother's happiness broke like sticks of furniture, hurled from the windows of an ancient house, dying with shame, burning to rags and fragments of bone his sisters and brothers. This oldest son, he threw himself on a funeral pyre of his own making, crying for his mother's hand, holding it as they leapt together, cursing every ancestor that charmed them into living, leaving his father to grieve alone.

The forest buried their remains. It forgot them. It returned to its first shape.

The father banished himself. Yet it was he chose to work as a woodcutter near that very spot of great destruction. He remembered all those, who, if they had been spared, would ask him all these questions. Who was who? Where do we come from? Why be here, slaving all the hours sent to you, drinking tea with sugar, dining on bread too fancy for our like, dreaming of our family and they all consumed by – consumed by what? Was it fire?

Fire.

My father, fire?

Fire, Father.

First published 2017 by Brandon,
an imprint of The O'Brien Press Ltd,
12 Terenure Road East, Rathgar,
Dublin 6, D06 HD27, Ireland
Tel: +353 1 4923333; Fax: +353 1 4922777
Email: books@obrien.ie
Website: www.obrien.ie
The O'Brien Press is a member of Publishing Ireland.

ISBN: 978-1-84717-907-4

10 9 8 7 6 5 4 3 2 1
22 21 20 19 18 17

Printed and bound by Gutenberg Press, Malta.
The paper in this book is produced using pulp from managed forests.

A NOTE ON THE COVER
When I was approaching the cover of *The Woodcutter and His Family*, I had in mind the
bridge, as it were, that James Joyce's work now is, between an older literary tradition and
a new one, and found we were immediately presented with the chance to do something
letterpress-inspired. And so I decided to mix a serif (Caslon) with a sans serif (Frutiger)
wooden-cut typeface. The serif represents traditional letterform and the sans signals a
modernist typeface. The work was carried out in The Print Museum, Dublin, in May
2017 with the assistance of Mary Plunkett and Declan Behan. The concept, coupled
with different printing processes, gives a special resonance to the imagery.

Emma Byrne, designer

Published in

The Woodcutter and His Family receives financial
assistance from the Arts Council